Do the Blind Dream?

Do the Blind Dream?

NEW NOVELLAS AND STORIES

BARRY GIFFORD

SEVEN STORIES PRESS

New York • London • Toronto • Melbourne

Seven Stories Press
140 Watts Street
New York, NY 10013
http://www.sevenstories.com/

IN CANADA

Hushion House, 36 Northline Road, Toronto, Ontario M4B 3E2

IN THE UK

Turnaround Publisher Services Ltd., Unit 3, Olympia Trading Estate, Coburg Road,
Wood Green, London N22 6TZ

IN AUSTRALIA

Palgrave Macmillan, 627 Chapel Street, South Yarra VIC 3141

LIBRARY OF CONGRESS CATALOGING-IN-PUBLICATION DATA
Gifford, Barry, 1946–
Do the blind dream? : new novellas and stories / Barry Gifford.
—A Seven Stories Press 1st ed.
p. cm.
ISBN 1-58322-635-4 (alk. paper)
I. Title.
PS3557.I283 D6 2004
813'.54—dc22
2003027063

College professors may order examination copies of Seven Stories Press titles
for a free six-month trial period. To order, visit www.sevenstories.com/textbook/
or fax on school letterhead to 212.226.1411.

Book design by India Amos
Jacket design by POLLEN/Stewart Cauley

Printed in the USA

9 8 7 6 5 4 3 2 1

For Dan

. . .
. . .

Acknowledgments

"The Ciné" originally appeared in the magazine *Post Road* (New York, 2002). The first section of "Ball Lightning" originally appeared, in different form, in the novel *Wyoming* (New York, 2000). This version of "Ball Lightning" appeared in the magazine *First Intensity* (Lawrence, Kansas, 2003). "Life Is Like This Sometimes" originally appeared in the magazine *Oyster Boy Review* (San Francisco, 2003). "Rosa Blanca" originally appeared in the magazine *Film Comment* (New York, 2003).

The author wishes to express his gratitude to Daniel Schmid for his editorial expertise and participation in the composition of the story "Havana Moon."

Contents

Do the Blind Dream?

. . .
. . .

A NOVELLA

To that girl leaning
out the window, waving

"A kiss, a bite . . . one who truly loves with all her heart can easily mistake them."

—Heinrich von Kleist, *Penthesilea*

I

It was late afternoon in the bedroom of a house in Fùlmine, a small town close to the sea in the south of Italy. Punctuated by occasional thunder and lightning, rain punished the walls and pounded against a high window. The room was sparsely furnished: a bed, a dresser and a mirror. On the wall over the bed hung a crucifix. Fresh yellow and blue flowers stood stiffly in a vase on the dresser.

In the center of the room rested an open coffin in which lay the body of Beatrice, a woman seventy-six years old at the time of her death the day before. Her face, while not serene, was remarkably free of lines and wrinkles. Next to the coffin, seated in chairs, were two of the deceased woman's three children, Sandra and Aldo, who was barely a year older than his sister. Both of them were distraught, crying or between bouts of crying.

"Is Cara coming?" Sandra asked.

"Aunt Rosa spoke to her. She was filming in Spain. She'll be here before they close the coffin."

"Is Buddy with her?"

"Yes," said Aldo.

"Good. What time is that?"

"She had to wait until this morning to get a plane to Madrid from somewhere in the North. Then they fly from Madrid to Rome. From there they'll come by car."

"I meant," Sandra said, "what time do they close the coffin?"

"At six. Then we go to the church."

Sandra looked at her watch.

"It's only four-thirty. It'll destroy Cara if she's too late to see Mamma one last time."

"How long have Cara and Buddy been together?" Aldo asked.

"Two or three months, I think."

Aldo stood up and took one of his mother's hands in his own. He bent down and kissed her face, then her ringless hand before collapsing onto her body.

"Mamma! Mamma!" he cried.

Sandra rose and put an arm around her brother, hugging him. After a few moments he released his mother's hand and sat down again, as did Sandra.

"Is Papa going to come?" Aldo asked.

"He'd better not try."

"Rosa would kill him."

"I'll kill him."

Aldo wiped tears from his cheeks and eyes.

"You know," he said, "he came to see Mamma a couple of weeks ago."

"No, I didn't. Why? He hadn't seen her in years."

"Mamma asked to see him."

"Asked? She couldn't ask."

A large clap of thunder rocked the house, rattling the bedroom window.

"She spoke his name, over and over," said Aldo. "Rosa didn't want to, but she telephoned him and he came. Papa sat with Mamma for three hours. He sang their old songs, recited her favorite poems. I was here."

"Did she recognize him?"

"I think Mamma always knew what was happening. She was a prisoner inside her mind. I could see it in her eyes, behind her eyes."

"No," said Sandra, "I don't believe it. She was lost a long time ago. Fifteen years—twelve, at least."

"Cara told me Mamma spoke to Buddy."

"To Buddy? When was this?"

"It's true—the last time she visited, three weeks ago, Cara said she was sitting with Mamma on the couch, holding her, stroking her hair. Buddy was sitting in a chair across from Mamma, or standing, I don't know. All of a sudden, Mama looked directly at Buddy and said, 'Beautiful.' She turned and looked at Cara, then back at Buddy, and Mamma said to him, 'Poor guy.' Then she faded away again."

"No! That's fantastic!"

Aldo shook his head.

"Cara couldn't believe it, either. She said Buddy joked that Mamma felt sorry for him, and despite the sickness she had to warn him, to let him know she knew how difficult life would be for him with Cara."

"Unbelievable."

"Buddy met Papa, too, around the same time. Papa asked him how many children Buddy had, and Buddy told him two."

"Buddy has two children?"

"Apparently. Anyway, Papa said he had six, and Buddy said, 'But I'm not finished yet.' Buddy told me that Papa, eighty years old, sick, barely able to stand by himself, got a dark look in his eyes and said, 'I'm not, either.'"

Sandra grunted.

"He's sick, all right. He's always been sick."

Tears spilled suddenly from her eyes. Annoyed, she fished around in her pockets, found a fresh tissue, and quickly wiped them away.

"Papa had better not try to come," she said.

"He won't. Rosa hates him, and as long as you're here he knows he's not welcome."

Ignazio, Sandra's husband, and Giuliana, Aldo's wife, entered the bedroom and sat down next to their respective spouses.

"I mean it!" Sandra said. "I won't let that monster near Mamma."

"Papa's not a monster," said Aldo.

"You don't know him."

"He's my father, too. What do you mean, I don't know him?"

"You didn't know he had another family! A wife and a child."

Aldo shook his head.

"Nobody knew, not Mamma . . ."

"Of course, not Mamma!" Sandra shouted. "Just like she didn't know about all of his other women."

"Pretended not to know."

"He fucked every girl or woman he met, or tried to. Mamma couldn't keep a maid or a girl to help with us. He even did it with Gabriella."

Aldo stared at Sandra.

"How do you know this? Gabriella moved to Argentina thirty years ago."

"Why do you suppose Mamma would never mention the name of her only sister?"

"You know what happened. When Gabriella was twenty-five she was misdiagnosed with a blood disease and told she had only a short time to live, two or three years; so she went out and slept with every man in town. By the time she found out she wasn't going to die she'd disgraced herself in Fùlmine. That's why she had to marry a foreigner, because nobody here would have her."

Sandra laughed.

"Don't be a fool, Aldo. Cara and I know the truth."

"Where is Cara?" Ignazio asked.

"She's coming," said Aldo. "She and Buddy should be here any minute."

"Do they know the coffin will be sealed at six?" asked Sandra.

"They know."

Noises came from the other side of the apartment. They heard the doorbell ring, then the front door open and close, followed by a rush of voices. Rosa, who had been Beatrice's caregiver, and in whose apartment she had lived the last five years of her life, rushed into the bedroom.

"It's Cara," she said.

Immediately behind Rosa came Cara, followed by Buddy, her American boyfriend. Cara's face was a mess from crying, but her distress could not disguise her unique beauty. Cara went straight to the coffin and threw herself on Beatrice, sobbing loudly. Sandra and Aldo caressed and held her as Buddy stood in the doorway, watching.

"Mamma! Mamma!" Cara screamed. "No! No! Mamma!"

Sandra, Aldo and Giuliana's attempts to comfort Cara were futile. She was clearly inconsolable.

"I should have been here!"

"Aldo was with her," said Sandra, "and Rosa."

"She died in my arms," said Aldo.

"Oh, Mamma!" Cara cried.

Ignazio gently guided Cara to a chair. She allowed him to briefly embrace her. The others acknowledged Buddy's presence with embraces, kisses on the cheeks, handshakes.

"Thank goodness you're here, Buddy," said Sandra.

"Cara told me Beatrice stopped eating two days ago."

"She gave up before the Alzheimer's. When she found out about Donatella and little Silvio. He made her sick."

Aldo shook his head.

"Papa didn't cause the disease," he said.

"How do you know?" said Sandra. "She might have resisted it longer."

"Alzheimer's doesn't work that way."

"Maybe it wasn't even Alzheimer's," Sandra said. "She was never tested."

Ignazio came over to Buddy.

"It must have been a difficult time for you with Cara when Aldo called."

Buddy nodded.

"She knew it was coming, but she took it hard. Not ever having a chance to hear Beatrice tell her she loved her was devastating."

Aldo, hearing this, came over.

"My mother was not herself for so many years."

"I mean even before the Alzheimer's affected her," said Buddy. "Cara told me Beatrice never, or rarely, showed her any real affection."

"The situation was difficult, certainly," said Aldo.

Rosa came over to Buddy and took his hand.

"It's so good you're here," she said to him. "Without you, I don't know how Cara could stand it."

"I don't want to intrude. Cara insisted that I come."

"She'd be devastated if you hadn't. I could see when you were here before how quickly and deeply Cara had become attached to you. She believes in you, Buddy, don't disappoint her."

"I'll do my best, Rosa. But you know, it works both ways."

"Cara is very nervous," said Rosa, "but she's a good girl. And she loves you."

Sandra was sitting next to Cara, holding her younger sister close. Cara struggled to compose herself.

"I never sleep, Sandra. I think I won't be able to really rest until I'm dead, too."

"It's Papa's fault, all of it. If I ever see him again, I'm going to put his eyes out."

Cara pulled away, sat up and fixed the clips in her hair.

"You'll make me crazy, Sandra. Don't say that! In front of Mamma."

"He's a devil," said Sandra. "Admit it and you'll be able to sleep."

"Sandra, no. He was the one who loved me, not Mamma. When I was three years old one day Mamma was angry at me for something—I wouldn't eat, probably—and Papa came home. She told him what a bad girl I was, and he picked me up and held me and told me that before I was born I'd been an angel. He caressed my back and shoulders and said, 'Cara, my little angel, here's where your wings used to be.' It's why I can forgive him, for everything."

"Don't be stupid, Cara. He's insane."

Cara stood up.

"Not now, Sandra, don't! Not with Mamma like this."

Sandra shrugged her shoulders.

"She can't hear us."

"How do you know she can't? Nobody knows anything about the dead, not even if they're really dead."

"Who's the crazy one?"

"Everybody in this family's crazy, Sandra. Don't you see it?"

"How does Buddy put up with you?"

"Don't talk about Buddy! He's not your man."

Buddy and Aldo looked at Cara and Sandra, then resumed talking quietly with Ignazio.

Cara stood up and went over to the coffin. Giuliana guided a chair under her and Cara sat down and stroked Beatrice's hands. Sandra got up and walked out of the room. Ignazio followed her.

Two men from the funeral home entered the bedroom, dressed in dark suits. One of them was carrying a hammer and a small paper bag, both of which he placed on the bureau.

"In a few minutes we'll seal the coffin," he said.

Cara exploded in tears. Aldo rushed over and held her.

"Not yet, not yet," said the man from the funeral home. "We can wait a little longer."

He and his companion left the bedroom.

"Remember when you were a kid," Aldo said to Cara, "and I sold you to my friends? I was twelve or thirteen."

"Sold me?"

Aldo grinned.

"I was so ashamed later. That's why I gave you the money."

"I don't think . . ."

"You were seven. I made you pull up your dress and pull down your pants. They wanted to see a girl's pussy. None of us had seen one except in a picture in a magazine. I told you to do it and you did. You don't remember?"

"Not really, no."

"My friends were very disappointed because you didn't have any hair down there. They said it wasn't a real pussy."

Cara and Aldo laughed together. He took out a handkerchief and dried her tears.

"A couple of the boys asked for their money back," he said, "but I refused. They got angry but I was bigger than they were. Nobody wanted to fight me."

Cara kissed Aldo on the cheek and he held her close.

"Do you think Mamma knows we're here?" Cara asked.

"I knew this would be tough, Cara, but it's even tougher than I thought."

Beatrice sat up in her coffin. She looked around at the people in the room, her gaze lingering for several long seconds on each person, none of whom noticed her. The last person she fixed on was Cara. Then she spoke.

"So many tears wasted on the dead. But who am I to criticize? How many thousands of times did I want to cry while I was captive in my own body? And now that I've been released I have even less freedom. No freedom at all, in fact. Being dead is not like the nuns and priests tell you. But they're no worse than anyone else, and no worse off. If I could help my children, I would. Poor babies. The longer they live the more they'll suffer. They're only beginning to understand."

The two men from the funeral home entered again. One of them picked up the coffin lid which had been leaning against one wall. The other picked up the hammer and shook several nails from the paper bag.

"It's time," he said to Aldo and Cara.

Cara continued crying but stood and caressed her mother, who remained sitting up, her eyes wide open. Aldo did the same. As they were doing this, Sandra came in, walked over to the coffin and kissed Beatrice. The three of them then walked out of the room, accompanied by Buddy and Giuliana.

One of the funeral men placed a hand on Beatrice's right shoulder. She patted it with her own hand.

"I know, I know," she said, "I heard him. I won't give you a hard time."

Rosa walked into the bedroom smoking a cigarette. She stopped and stared at Beatrice.

"Rosa, give me a drag, will you?"

Rosa walked over and handed her cigarette to Beatrice. Beatrice puffed on it, inhaled deeply, then exhaled. She handed the cigarette back to Rosa.

"Thanks," Beatrice said.

Rosa kissed her, then stood back a little to allow the men from the funeral home to do their work. She wiped the tears from her face. Beatrice lay back down in the coffin. One of the men placed the coffin lid over her, and then the other nailed it shut.

2

It was early evening. The coffin containing Beatrice's corpse was carried out the door of the house by the two men from the funeral home, Aldo, Ignazio and Buddy, and loaded into the back of a black hearse. The two funeral workers got into the car and proceeded very slowly toward the church as the family followed behind, walking in the middle of the street. A light but persistent rain fell. Neighbors and passersby observed the procession, most crossing themselves as it went by. Cara and Aldo walked directly behind the hearse, followed by Sandra with Buddy, then Ignazio with Giuliana and Rosa.

"My mother was very beautiful once," said Sandra. "Did you know that? Did Cara ever show you photographs of Beatrice as a young woman?"

"A few, yes," Buddy said. "She was striking."

"You can't imagine how that man tortured her. If she hadn't been a Catholic, I'm certain she would have committed suicide."

"You mean Massimo?"

"The world would have been better off had my father never been born."

"Then I wouldn't have you," said Ignazio.

"You'd be better off, too," Sandra said to him. "Don't be a hypocrite. You've said it yourself many times."

"Stop this!" Aldo said. "With Mamma in her coffin, can't you quit bitching?"

Giuliana patted her husband's arm.

"Everybody's upset, Aldo. It's difficult for us all."

"Think of how Beatrice is on her way to heaven now," said Rosa. "She's with the saints." Rosa crossed herself.

Beatrice appeared, trailing the others. She stopped in the street as a man came walking toward her.

"Do you have a cigarette?" Beatrice asked him.

The man stopped, pulled a pack of cigarettes from one of his pockets, shook one out and gave it to her. He took out a lighter and lit the cigarette for Beatrice, who inhaled deeply.

"Thank you," she said. "You never know when it might be the last one."

"I always smoke each cigarette as if it were," he answered. "That way I enjoy it even more."

The man put the pack of cigarettes and his lighter back into his pocket, nodded politely, and walked on. Beatrice stood there, smoking.

"Massimo, my husband," she said, "was impotent when we were married. He told me he'd never been able to have proper relations with a woman. His sister, Claudia, ruined him, he said. Claudia the famous painter, seven years older than Massimo. She made him show her his cock when he was ten or eleven years old, and told him he would never be able to satisfy a woman, not with such a small penis. For some reason, he believed her.

"She was a terrible woman, really terrible. Her first husband, a Spanish writer, killed himself after four years with Claudia. Hanged himself from a chandelier in their hotel room in Barcelona. Her second husband, Gatti, the cellist, could get an erection only by watching Claudia make love with another man. She told me.

"Claudia made Massimo masturbate in front of her and as soon as his little cock got hard she would suck it until he came in her mouth.

This began when he was twelve. She told him he would probably be a homosexual, fit only to suck other men's cocks—as if this were such a terrible thing. Even after she had married Javier, Claudia continued this horrible game with Massimo. Javier must have discovered it. Perhaps he didn't, I'm not certain. God only knows how Claudia chose to torture him. Once she had a man in her thrall the only way out for him was suicide, a mortal sin. This way Claudia would take not only their lives but their souls, too. Gatti shot himself one night while she had two men at the same time, sucking one while the other fucked her in the ass. This was the activity she preferred. Massimo said he watched Claudia do it when he was sixteen.

"The public loved her, of course. Claudia's art was revered around the world by the time she was thirty. She was like a movie star. She looked like one, with long wavy, blue-black hair, an enormous mouth and a great figure; tits not too big, prominent ass, nice legs. Her nose was too big, but it made her bold, daring anyone to criticize her, as if she were always ready to attack, which she was. A phenomenon. The tragic deaths of her husbands created sympathy for her from the people. There was no cruelty in her paintings, only tenderness, a quality she could never convey in real life. Tenderness in her extraordinary use of light, Tuscan light, the light she captured from her childhood.

"It took almost one year for Massimo and I to consummate our marriage. He claimed it was a miracle. Only after praying to Saint Anthony could he perform properly. Anthony, the patron saint of lovers. In a way, I wish he had remained impotent, because after this Massimo had no self-control when it came to sex, no judgment. He wanted to make love all the time, but not just to me, to every woman or girl who would have him. Massimo must even have slept with many of his female students at the college. And then there was Donatella, his mistress. Making up for lost time, I guess, and to take his revenge in his way on Claudia—except I was the one who suffered.

"But he never could really have his revenge on her, this I know. She told me that he tried to make love to her once, years later, while she was married to Gatti. He bragged to his sister about his many conquests, telling her how wrong she'd been, what a masterful seducer and cocksman he had become despite her deviltry. Show me, Claudia demanded, challenging him. She undressed, lay down in front of him and spread her legs. He tried, she told me, but he couldn't. Massimo's cock was dead in her presence. No matter what he did, he couldn't get an erection. She shoved her big ass in his face and laughed at him. He beat her then, Claudia said, beat her badly, until she bled. Called her a witch. When she didn't try to stop him, Massimo cried, then begged her forgiveness. Can you imagine?

"It was the last time they saw each other. She and Gatti moved to New York soon thereafter, and she never returned to Italy. Claudia was fond of saying in interviews that Italian society was burned out, she was happier in the new world. I wouldn't know about any of this, since I never traveled out of the country. Claudia died ten years ago, of breast cancer.

"Oh, well, I suppose I shouldn't keep them waiting."

Beatrice took a final puff on her cigarette, dropped it, stepped on the butt, and began walking in the same direction as the funeral procession.

3

Seated in the first pew of the church were the family: Cara, Aldo, Sandra, Ignazio, Giuliana, Rosa and Buddy. Beatrice was seated in the row behind the family, at the end of the pew. The closed coffin was at the front of the church, on a pedestal, strewn with floral bouquets. Next to it was a podium. Friends and relations of the family were seated throughout the church. The mourners sat quietly, a few whispering to each other. A priest entered from a door to one side of the coffin, walked to the podium and stood behind it. Before speaking, he stared—glared—at the son and daughters of the dead woman seated in the front row.

"Beatrice would be astonished to see her children here today," he said. "It took her death to bring them into God's home. It took her death. And this woman, we are certain, having made her peace with Our Father, is safe in Heaven now."

There was movement at the back of the church. A woman approximately Beatrice's age entered, dressed eccentrically: half-formal, half-slovenly, a large, feathered hat. She seemed oblivious to the somber mood of the proceedings, chatting gaily to those seated in aisle seats as she made her way toward the front of the church. It was Camilla, Beatrice's cousin. She shook several hands during her procession. When she came to Beatrice, Camilla looked at her curiously, as if she could not quite place the dead woman, who nodded and smiled courteously to Camilla before returning her attention to the priest. Camilla took a seat.

"Safe and free," declared the priest, "the kind and gentle Beatrice. It is her children who have failed to make their peace with Him. To them, I say, better to go to your homes after apologizing to your sainted mother, and kill yourselves. Not being Catholic is your greatest sin—suicide, in this case, is the only honorable act left to you."

Aldo stood up and shook his fist at the priest.

"How dare you speak this way over the dead body of our mother?!" he shouted. "I'll punch your god damn lights out!"

Ignazio took hold of Aldo, preventing him from going after the priest. Sandra also stood and stared defiantly at him. Cara seemed confused, dazed by the concomitant events, still crying. The priest stared righteously at Aldo and Sandra, unflinching. Beatrice betrayed no particular emotion at this turn in the events. Camilla stood up and began shaking hands with people, speaking to them as she moved around the room.

"My taxi must be here by now," said Camilla, "I have to go . . .

"It's so good to see you again, but you've really aged, haven't you? . . .

"Our mother wouldn't leave us on our own until we were fourteen years old. Don't you think that was being overly cautious? . . .

"Beatrice was far too generous with her children; they're very rich, you know . . .

"My taxi's here, I'm going . . ."

Camilla prattled on as she walked a bit unsteadily toward the exit. Aldo and Sandra sat down again, as the priest continued.

"In these last few weeks I spent many hours in the company of the departed, and I am certain, even though her ability to communicate was impaired, dear Beatrice lamented the fact that she was alone in her faith among her family. She felt this isolation acutely, and indeed was damaged by it."

"What the hell is he talking about?" Aldo whispered loudly to Ignazio, then yelled at the priest, "What the hell are you saying? You didn't know my mother!"

"He came to the house a few times," Rosa whispered to Sandra and Cara. "Perhaps once every ten days in the last two months. I gave him tea and cookies. When he'd finished them, he'd bless Beatrice, then leave. Twenty minutes each visit, no more."

Beatrice stood up, then slowly walked up to her coffin and stood behind it next to the priest, who suddenly froze in his malevolent stance and expression directed at Aldo, Sandra and Cara. Beatrice took out a handkerchief and wiped perspiration from the priest's forehead. He remained frozen in place. She looked out at the room. Everyone was frozen except for her cousin, Camilla, who at this moment re-entered the church and wandered through the aisles, chattering indecipherably to herself. Finally, Camilla took a seat at the front, looked at Beatrice and spoke directly to her.

"Massimo came to see me after you were married. I never told you. He said I was the one he really wanted, but that he'd always been too shy to ask me, afraid I'd laugh at him and send him away. Remember, Beatrice, what beautiful long blonde hair I had in those days? Blonde hair was so rare in the South."

"When was this?" asked Beatrice.

"A few months after your wedding. Massimo said he knew it had been a mistake, taking you while his heart belonged to me."

"Did he make love to you?"

"Oh, no," Camilla laughed, "he couldn't."

"Couldn't?"

"I was a virgin. I still am. I was keeping myself for my husband, only I never found one. Have I missed something?"

"Tell me, Camilla, were you ever in love, or thought you were?"

"I don't think so, not really. Honestly, I could never imagine what people meant when they talked about love. They looked stupid or insane or both when they did. I didn't want to act like that."

"No, Camilla, you didn't miss anything."

Camilla stood up.

"I'm very glad to hear it," she said. "My taxi's here."

Camilla began walking toward the door.

Beatrice said, "It was good to see you, Camilla."

Camilla waved back at her and left the church for the second time.

Beatrice looked at the priest.

"You wouldn't happen to have a cigarette on you?" she asked.

The priest's mouth unfroze.

"In my left pants pocket," he said.

Beatrice reached into the priest's pocket and pulled out a pack of cigarettes and a lighter. She took one and lit up, then replaced the pack and the lighter in his pocket.

"Why isn't Massimo here?" she said. "In the end, he's the one who matters most to me, and I hate myself for feeling this way. He took my family money to start his business and never repaid it; betrayed me countless times with other women; committed bigamy, then abandoned me. So why can I not free myself from him in death any more than I could while I was alive?"

The priest coughed, straightened up, took out his cigarettes, lit one and smoked it as he walked away toward his office. Aldo got up from his seat and went after him. Sandra nudged Ignazio, who got up and followed them. Sandra remained seated.

Beatrice stared at the coffin, then addressed herself.

"You seemed to be a smart girl once, but you never were, not at all. For example, you believed that in heaven nobody told a lie. Is there a heaven other than this? I wish somebody had figured out during my lifetime what truth really is. I've always thought that the afterlife was a place where nobody was too happy or too sad, everything just sort of without strong feelings. I wonder if I'm there yet.

"Massimo never worried about whether or not there was an afterlife. I don't think he ever believed in it or cared. He behaved so badly during our life together that it's hard for me to really understand how I endured it, although he was a good provider and very entertaining at times. I mostly ignored the fact of his mistresses. Perhaps I shouldn't have but that wasn't my mistake. It was the other thing. If there is a living hell, I guess he's in it."

Sandra stood up.

"Why did you pretend that nothing was happening?" she asked Beatrice. "A mother is supposed to protect her children."

Beatrice shook her head.

"There was nobody to protect me," she said, then stubbed her cigarette out on the coffin lid.

Everybody else, including Sandra, got up and filed slowly out of the church until Beatrice was the only one left.

4

After the funeral, Aldo, Sandra, Ignazio, Giuliana, Cara, Buddy and Rosa were all in the living room of Rosa's house. Beatrice came in and stood leaning against a wall near the doorway.

Aldo began pacing back and forth across the room.

"I'll never forgive myself for not ripping the ears off his stupid head," he said.

"You don't hit a priest," said Giuliana.

"You don't have anything to say in this," Sandra told her. "Aldo should have hit him. The priest was talking shit."

"He had no right to tell us to go home and kill ourselves," said Aldo.

"Is that what he said?" asked Cara.

Sandra stared at her sister.

"You were there, you heard him."

"I couldn't listen," said Cara, "I was too upset."

Aldo stopped in front of Ignazio, who was sitting on the couch, and said, "You should have let me beat the crap out of him."

"Who was that strange woman coming in and out and talking to everyone?" Ignazio asked.

"Cousin Camilla," said Sandra. "At one time she and Mamma were very close. When they were girls."

"Is she crazy?" said Ignazio.

"Not really," Aldo said. He sat down next to his brother-in-law. "A little eccentric, that's all."

"She never married," said Sandra. "Camilla lives in her own little world. And you," she said to Buddy, "Mr. Visitor from Another Planet. All of this must seem very strange to you, eh? Do people behave like this in America?"

"Death is always a shock," Buddy said, "even when you know it's coming."

"That priest was out of line," said Ignazio. "Maybe I shouldn't have stopped Aldo."

Buddy nodded and said, "If I had understood what he was saying, I would have jumped him myself."

"The children have never been religious," said Aldo. "Superstitious, yes, but Sandra and Cara and I weren't raised Catholic. Mamma was, but our father despised the Catholic church. His heroes were Gramsci and Lumumba."

Beatrice took a cigarette from an open pack lying on a table. Aldo then picked one from the pack and took out his lighter. As he was about to light his cigarette, Giuliana spoke to him.

"Aldo, what should we do about dinner?"

Aldo held the lighter flame open and Beatrice leaned down and lit her cigarette.

"We can all go to Rocco's," Aldo told his wife.

Aldo lit his cigarette, then put away his lighter. Beatrice sat down in a chair.

Giuliana said, "I'll call and see if we can reserve a table."

"I need to lie down for a few minutes," said Cara. She stood up. "Buddy, will you come with me?"

"Sure, baby."

"I'll fix the bed for you," Rosa said.

Rosa, Cara and Buddy left the room together.

"All right, Aldo," said Sandra, "what about the money?"

"The money? You mean Mamma's money?"

"What other money would I be talking about? Mamma had a life insurance policy."

"Sure, she did. We'll split it up four ways."

"Four ways? You, Cara and me. Who's the fourth?"

"Aunt Rosa."

"You're joking! Rosa doesn't deserve an equal share. She doesn't deserve anything, really."

"Sandra, what are you talking about? She took care of Mamma all these years."

"She was paid for it."

"She loved Mamma, the same as us."

"She never loved Mamma. I don't believe that. She wouldn't have been so kind unless we'd been paying her."

"Sandra, you're terrible. Rosa was closer to Mamma than anyone."

"She's not a sincere person."

Aldo puffed on his cigarette, then put it out in an ashtray. Thunder rumbled in the distance.

"Aldo, we'll give her something, but not one-fourth. How much is there, anyway?"

"About seventy thousand dollars."

"Give her four thousand. That leaves us twenty-two apiece."

"I'd rather give her ten. Let's ask Cara what she thinks."

"Cara will go along with you, you know it. She can't deal with money. A thousand dollars or a hundred thousand dollars, it's gone like a cool breeze. Just like her men."

"Buddy seems to be a pretty stable guy."

"He probably is. All the more reason why as soon as he gets enough of what's between her legs and comes up for air, he'll take one look around and head for the border."

"I'd like to see Cara be really happy for a change. She's not so nervous when Buddy's around."

"I'd like to see her happy, too, Aldo. I'm not such a monster. I just think she's afraid of trusting any man, so she destroys a relationship that threatens to go too well, before it can really work."

"We'll give Aunt Rosa seven thousand, then. That leaves each of us twenty-one. All right?"

"All right."

"I'm ready for a drink."

Aldo got up and went over to a table that had liquor bottles and glasses on it. He poured drinks for himself and Sandra, brought them over and handed one to her. They tapped glasses and drank.

Beatrice sat and stared at them.

"What do I have a right to expect from my children?" she said. "Nothing now, certainly. Dead people have no rights. When they were growing up, Aldo was the easiest of the three for me. We always had a good relationship. Perhaps because he was a boy, he felt protective of his mother. The girls, especially Sandra, were competitive with me for their father's affection. I suppose this is normal, but Massimo seemed almost to encourage this behavior. I have to admit it colored my feelings.

"I'm sure both Cara and Sandra felt that I wasn't as attentive to them as I might have been. I regret this now. Cara needed me at a very important time and I wasn't able to bring myself to help her. Sandra has always been tougher than Cara, more capable of taking care of herself. Even she could see it, as a teenager—she told me to protect Cara, but I couldn't do it. I was in denial. Maybe this was what caused my 'condition.'"

Ignazio, Giuliana and Rosa came into the room.

"Sandra and I are having a drink," Aldo said to them. "Would you like something?"

Ignazio poured drinks for himself and Giuliana and Rosa. Beatrice stood up and walked out.

5

Aldo, Sandra, Buddy, Cara, Giuliana and Ignazio
were seated at a table in Rocco's, a small, modest restaurant in Fùlmine.
Food and wine were on the table.

"Cara," Aldo said, "you can't mean that."

"Of course, I do. If you hadn't married Giuliana, she would have had
to find an American to take her, like Gabriella."

"Gabriella went to Buenos Aires," said Sandra.

"It's the same," Cara replied.

"You're the one with the American," Giuliana said to Cara, "not me.
And if you're calling me a whore, we'll have to invent a new word for
what you are."

"Stop it, both of you," said Ignazio. "This is crazy."

Cara turned on him.

"Do you think Sandra is happy? Ask her. She calls up crying all the
time."

"Cara, calm down," Buddy said. "Everyone is tense tonight."

Giuliana stood up and turned to go. Aldo tried to take her arm, but
she shook away his hand.

"Giuliana, sit down," he said.

"I won't listen to her any more," Giuliana said. "Beatrice's death is no excuse for her behavior. You're a spoiled girl, Cara. Spoiled and sick."

"I've been working since I was seventeen," said Cara, "supporting myself all these years. Nobody ever gave me anything."

"You're a selfish child, the most self-absorbed person I've ever met."

"Giuliana!" barked Aldo. "That's enough."

"You're just jealous," Cara spat at Giuliana.

"Of whom? Of you? The movie star? Because you fucked every director and actor in Europe?"

"You're the one who fucked everybody," said Cara. "You're jealous of me and any other woman who has children. I'm not to blame for your infertility, or your frigidity."

"Cara, really," said Buddy.

"I know all about you, Giuliana," Cara said.

Giuliana looked at Buddy, then back at Cara.

"Listen to your dream girl, Buddy," she said. "Look at her. The princess. Isn't she elegant. She'll turn on you, too, you'll see. She's a snake."

Giuliana walked out of the restaurant.

"You can't stand the truth!" Cara shouted after her.

Aldo stood up.

"I won't forgive you for this, Cara. It wasn't necessary."

He followed his wife.

Sandra shook her head and said to Cara, "You went too far."

"She had no right to say anything to Buddy."

"You're lucky Aldo didn't hit you," said Ignazio.

Sandra laughed. "She would have liked it. Cara likes to be beaten, doesn't she, Buddy? She needs it."

Cara's eyes filled with tears.

"What do you know about what I need? What does anybody know?"

Cara walked out. Sandra went after her.

Ignazio picked up his glass of wine and held it up toward Buddy.

"Welcome to the family," Ignazio said.

Buddy picked up his glass of wine and clinked it gently against Ignazio's. They drank.

6

The church was empty until Massimo entered from the rear. He was slightly stooped and shuffled forward toward the coffin, which still rested on a platform behind the podium. When he arrived at the bier, Massimo stood next to it and placed one of his hands on the box. He looked around to see if he was alone before he spoke.

"I never thought you would die before I did. Even with the Alzheimer's. You were such a beautiful girl, Beatrice, a beautiful woman. That wasn't you at Rosa's, that wasn't even a woman."

The priest appeared, smoking a cigarette. When he saw Massimo, he stopped. They stared at one another.

"This is not your house," said the priest.

"I'm saying goodbye to my wife."

"She wasn't your wife for the last twenty years. You abandoned Beatrice, divorced her. Conceived children in sin."

"I'm a man."

"Not in God's eyes."

"You've been blinded by Him."

The two funeral workers came in, one of them pushing a handtruck. They approached the priest.

"We're ready to take the coffin for cremation," said the one without the handtruck.

"Go ahead," said the priest.

The two men wheeled the coffin out of the church. Massimo and the priest watched them go. Then Massimo turned and looked at the priest.

"You were always a prick, John," he said, "even when we were kids."

"Only God could have mercy on your soul," the priest replied, and walked away.

Massimo shouted at his back, "Tell Him not to bother."

Massimo began to walk slowly out of the church. Suddenly, he stopped, put one hand to his chest, and collapsed to the ground. A well-preserved older woman appeared. She walked over to where Massimo was lying on the floor and looked down at him.

"Get up, Massimo. Come on, you can do it."

Massimo stirred, then ran his hands over his body. He opened his eyes and saw her.

"My God, Claudia. But you're dead."

"So are you. Get up."

Massimo slowly climbed to his feet. He brushed dust off of his clothes.

"What do you mean, I'm dead? I'm standing here, talking to you."

"That's right, you're talking to me."

"Jesus."

"Don't try to figure it out. I'm much more intelligent than you are and I haven't been able to."

"I always thought, if there really is a hell, that's where you were."

"If hell existed, I'd be there. And now you, too."

"I must have had a heart attack. Is that what killed me?"

"What difference does it make?"

"For Christ's sake, Claudia! I just want to know what happened."

Claudia caressed Massimo's face with one of her hands, then walked a few steps away, looked at him, and said, "What happened is that your selfishness destroyed other people's lives. So did mine. That's why we're here. Wherever here is."

"You mean Beatrice."

"Beatrice, certainly. And Cara."

"I loved Cara."

"You're a monster, Massimo."

"If I'm a monster, then you're a sick old bitch!"

Claudia walked back toward him and stopped three feet away.

"Look at me, little brother. You're a lot older than I am."

"That's only because I lived longer. You're still a witch, Claudia."

"A witch or a bitch—which?"

She laughed and began again to walk away but halted when Beatrice appeared in her path.

"Hello, Claudia," Beatrice said. "I wasn't sure if I would see you or not."

"We don't really belong together, do we?"

"Beatrice," said Massimo, "I sang to you before you died. Do you remember?"

"I remember everything. It's terrible."

Massimo moved closer to Beatrice.

"Not everything," he said. "We had good times. We had the children."

"Massimo, stop it," said Claudia. "Don't embarrass yourself."

He turned on Claudia.

"It's because of you that I behaved the way I did."

Claudia laughed.

"How stupid," she said. "You can't use me as an excuse. Beatrice should have left you—or had you murdered."

"Beatrice loved me. Beatrice, you did love me, didn't you?"

"It's too late for this," Beatrice said.

"For this or anything else," said Claudia.

The priest appeared again. Massimo lay down on the floor in the same position and in the same spot where he had fallen. The priest saw him, hesitated, then knelt down next to Massimo and touched his hands and face. The priest crossed himself, stood up and hurried away.

"I was always puzzled by the ways in which other people behaved," said Beatrice. "Unlike you, Claudia, I was never able to truly embrace life. I was too shy and depressed much of the time."

"The truth is, Beatrice," Claudia replied, "that life is not for everyone."

Claudia took Beatrice by the arm and together they walked out of the church, leaving Massimo alone, lying on the floor.

"Beatrice!" he shouted.

7

Buddy and Cara were in her mother's room in Rosa's house, lying a couple of feet apart on Beatrice's bed. A small lamp burned on a bedside table. The rain had stopped.

"You were pretty hard on Giuliana," Buddy said.

"Yes, I know. I lost control a little bit."

"I knew the first time I saw you my life would never be the same."

"That night."

"You looked like a beautiful wreck."

"That's the first time anyone ever called me that, a wreck."

"I could see that you were in trouble. Anyone could."

"Certainly, I was. I was in a bad marriage and I didn't know how to get out of it. My children were suffering. My husband threatened to throw them out of a window and then strangle me."

"Was he suicidal?"

"No. He doesn't have that much courage."

"So, what happened?"

"I had a breakdown. For two years I didn't sleep. I drank too much, I worked a lot, so I felt guilty about leaving my children. They were in school, I couldn't always take them with me to where the movie was being shot. They stayed with the woman who worked for us in the house."

"And what about your husband? Where was he?"

"Working, too, mostly in France. He's very popular there."

"And when you were with him?"

"It was always a disaster. No, that's not entirely true. Sometimes, especially early in the twelve years we were together, he could be tender to me and kind to the children. But most of the time he was insecure, he felt he wasn't good enough for me, so he shouted, got crazy and sometimes violent."

"He hit you?"

"Several times. Once, in front of the children, he broke my nose and they attacked him. There was blood all over my clothes. Poor little girls, they couldn't stop crying. I called the police and he ran out of the house. They came and took me to the hospital."

"What happened to him?"

"Nothing, I didn't file charges. He apologized, he cried. It was the same every time."

"Why didn't you take the kids and go? Especially after he threatened to throw them out of a window?"

"It was stupid of me not to, I know. I tried, in my own way, to make it work."

"Did you have lovers?"

"Not for the first six years. Then I became so unhappy. I needed something, someone. I didn't have anything serious until the last couple of years, and even then I rarely saw the man. He wanted to marry me, to have a child, which he'd never had. He was my age but I wasn't really in love—for me, it was an escape."

"Your husband was older?"

"By eighteen years. When we began he promised to take care of me entirely, to make life easier for me and my daughter, who was only three years old. Her father never gave us anything. He didn't have any money and I didn't ask him."

"You were married before?"

"Yes. We lived together for five years, on and off. He preferred men, as it turned out. He's not a bad guy, just damaged. His father was terrible to him and he was an alcoholic by the time he was fourteen."

"He never supported his daughter?"

"No. He lives in Miami now, with a rich director and the director's mother in a big house. I don't know who sleeps with whom. It's a mysterious arrangement."

"You had a child by your second husband pretty quickly."

"I became pregnant before the marriage. I wasn't sure about having the baby, about having a child with him, but I wanted more children. I'd had two abortions by that time because I hadn't been certain of the fathers. There was a period during which I slept with many men, even while I was living with the father of my oldest daughter. We both fucked around a lot. It was stupid. He liked to watch me having sex with other men. Actually, it was the men he liked to watch, not me."

"You went along with this?"

"For a while. I didn't have a real love and in the beginning it excited me to be with more than one man at a time. My first husband directed everything. After a few times I started to hate it and finally I wouldn't do it any more. We split up soon after this. He went to Paris for a while and left me with the baby in Rome."

"What did you do then?"

"I was very poor but I got lucky. I was cast in a film that received a lot of attention, *The Last Huntress*. Since I had the feature role and people liked me as a kind of naive but tough girl, also pretty, which didn't hurt, I was able to build a career and support myself. My most terrible mistake was my second marriage. Even my father felt sorry for me when he saw what kind of man I'd married—weak, violent, sick in his soul."

"Why 'even' your father?"

Beatrice came into the room. She walked to the window and looked out as she listened to Buddy and Cara talk.

"My father loved me too much," Cara said.

She lit a cigarette, shifted her position on the bed and tucked her legs underneath her.

"We've had a difficult relationship."

Buddy nodded and said, "Most people I know have a difficult time with their father. You say he loved you too much."

"He did love me, I'm sure of that. But he was insanely possessive. My mother didn't love me enough—that was another problem, or part of it, certainly. It was because she knew about my father's feeling towards me, what became a kind of obsession. She resented the preference he showed me over her."

Cara paused for a few moments. Buddy watched her as she sucked on the cigarette.

"And then," Cara said, "when I was fourteen, he came to my room almost every night, after my mother had fallen asleep. Or he thought she was asleep."

"He molested you."

"I'm not entirely certain what he did. I'm sure that some defense mechanism in my mind prevents me from remembering precisely what happened. He would always caress my back and shoulders, especially my shoulder blades. I've told you this, haven't I? 'You're my little angel,' he'd whisper into my ear, 'and here's where your wings used to be.'"

Cara put out her cigarette in an ashtray on the table next to the bed.

"I always slept on my stomach," she said. "I didn't want to see his face, to turn around. He did whatever it was from behind while I pretended to be unconscious. Once I heard my mother's voice, calling him from her bedroom, asking him where he was, what he was doing."

"Did he stop?"

Cara lay back against the pillows and closed her eyes.

"No," she said, "he didn't answer."

"Your mother didn't come looking for him?"

"Never."

"She must have known what was happening."

Cara's eyes opened.

"Perhaps, but she didn't want to know."

Beatrice turned and looked at Cara.

"Of course I knew," said Beatrice.

"Jesus, Cara, how long did this go on?" asked Buddy. "His nightly visits."

"Until I was seventeen."

"What stopped him?"

"I began dating. He went crazy at first. He didn't want to allow a boy into the house. My mother did say something about this and he had to back down. I left home that same year. Moved to Rome and shared an apartment with another girl."

"Did your father come to see you there?"

"Oh, Buddy, I don't remember. Maybe once. He had a mistress, unknown to my mother and me, with whom he had had a son, who was two years old by the time I moved away. My father left my mother six months after I went to Rome, divorced her and married Donatella. They're still married, with three sons."

"And your mother?"

"She never took another man. At least I never heard about it if she did. She lived alone, then she got sick."

"How often do you see your father?"

"Once a year, maybe less. He and his wife come to Rome around Christmas, and if the kids and I are there they'll drop in. The time I saw him with you was an exception. I haven't been alone with him since I was seventeen."

"Did you tell your husbands about him?"

"My second husband, not the first. Neither of them had much to do with him since we rarely met. As I said, despite what he did it was my father who loved me. It's my mother's love that I missed."

Buddy reached over and held one of her hands. Cara squeezed his hand, then pulled back her own.

"You seem to have handled all of this remarkably well," said Buddy.

"I have dreams sometimes, one in particular. My father—or some man whose face I never see—appears in front of me while I'm sleeping, or I'm supposed to be asleep, and puts his cock into my mouth. I gag and vomit on the floor next to the bed. My eyes are closed until

I look at the floor. Something's moving but it's trapped in this sticky, dark brown mess.

"The man is standing there by the bed. He has a big hard cock. I start to vomit again, I can't stop gagging. Then I wake up. I'm excited and my cunt is wet. If a man is with me I try to get him to fuck me. It's always the same."

"How often do you have this dream?"

"Once every two or three months."

Cara lit another cigarette.

"Have you had it since we've been together?"

"I think so."

Cara stared straight ahead of her as she smoked, not looking at Buddy.

"Do you think blind people dream?" she asked. "I mean, people who've never had sight in their lives?"

"I don't know. Maybe they hear or smell things."

"Sometimes I wish I'd been born blind."

Cara began to cry.

"Do you think that's a terrible thing to say?"

Buddy kissed her. Aldo appeared in the doorway.

"Hey, Buddy," Aldo said, "do you want to go to the bar with me and Ignazio?"

Buddy looked at Cara. She smiled while tears ran down her face.

"Go," she said.

"We'll be back soon," said Aldo.

Buddy got up and left with Aldo. Beatrice came over and sat on the bed next to Cara.

"I had to tell someone," Cara said.

"I understand," said Beatrice. "I didn't know how to deal with it."

"And Sandra?"

"He might have done the same with her. I'm not certain."

"He didn't care for Sandra so much."

"It's true, he always loved you more. Perhaps this is why I didn't—wouldn't—help you. Will you forgive me?"

Cara put her cigarette in the ashtray.

"Of course, Mamma. Can you hold me?"

Beatrice cradled Cara, rocking her gently.

"Mamma?"

"Yes?"

"Tell me you love me."

Beatrice kissed Cara on the forehead, then stood up.

"When you and Sandra were little girls," Beatrice said, beginning to pace as she spoke, "I took you together often to the same doctor I had gone to as a child. Every time for several years he would say to you and your sister, 'You two are very beautiful, but not as beautiful as your mother.' Then one day he looked at you and said to me, 'Beatrice, I have to tell you, this one will be more beautiful than you.' I felt like the wicked queen in *Snow White*, I was overwhelmed by an uncontrollable jealousy."

Beatrice stopped pacing and looked at her daughter before continuing to talk.

"It horrified me," Beatrice said, "and I tried to overcome it, but every time I looked at you I thought of his words. The doctor was a man I'd trusted my entire life, so I believed him, I knew he wouldn't lie to me. Because of this, I refused to allow you to have a certain . . . intimacy with me."

"Oh, Mamma."

"And when I recognized Massimo's obsession with you, I stopped trying."

"It hurt me, Mamma. It still hurts more than anything."

"We both hurt you, Massimo and I. And later I couldn't do anything about it. I was lost for all of those years."

Cara got up from the bed, went over to Beatrice and embraced her.

"Can you tell me now, Mamma?" asked Cara.

Beatrice began to cry, slowly at first, then harder. Cara held her.

"It's all right, Mamma, I love you. It's enough."

Cara kissed her mother, then released her, walked back to the bed and lay down. She fell asleep immediately. Beatrice watched her. Buddy and Sandra came into the room. Cara woke up.

Cara saw Buddy and said to him, "I thought you were at the bar."

"I was. Aldo and Ignazio are still there. I was worried about you, so I came back."

Buddy and Sandra sat down on the bed on either side of Cara.

"I fell asleep and had the strangest dream," said Cara. "Buddy, you were sitting in a chair reading a story to my mother. Somehow I knew that my father was dead, and my mother was dead, too, only I couldn't let her know that I knew she wasn't really still alive. She seemed so pleased to just be sitting here on this bed listening to you read. I sat down next to her and caressed and kissed her. Then I woke up."

"It's a good dream, Cara," said Sandra.

"I guess you've answered your own question," Buddy said.

At first Cara did not understand, then she nodded and laughed a little.

"What question?" asked Sandra.

Beatrice stood in front of Cara. Sandra and Buddy got up.

"We'll let you rest some more," said Buddy. "Call me if you need me."

He and Sandra left the room together.

"Don't be afraid of Buddy," said Beatrice. "He won't steal you from yourself."

"Thanks, Mamma. I'll try."

Beatrice sat down next to Cara and put her arms around her. She stroked her daughter's hair.

"Everybody dreams, Cara," Beatrice said. "Even the dead."

Ball Lightning

: : :

I

*It **was** late **afternoon*** of a late spring day. The rural two-lane next to which stood a two-pump filling station was empty. The faint sound of an approaching car could be heard, a dim buzz that became louder and louder until a sparkling new blue Ford Sunliner convertible with the top down pulled up at the pumps. A young blond woman sat behind the steering wheel. She pressed the horn several times, until an attendant emerged from the station garage. The attendant, dressed in grimy gray overalls and a red baseball cap, stepped around to the driver's side of the Ford.

"You must be in a hurry."

"Fill it up."

"Regular or ethyl?"

"Ethyl, I guess."

"Pretty automobile."

"I guess."

"Machine inside has soft drinks. Mostly Nehi. Grape, orange and root beer."

"Just fill it, okay?"

The attendant walked over to the ethyl pump, rotated the handle to activate it, took down the hose, unscrewed the Ford's gas cap, inserted the hose nozzle and began fueling the car.

"Hey," said the driver, "how far am I from Superior?"

"The lake?"

"No, the town."

"Forty, forty-five miles. But you won't get there this way."

"I thought this was the road to Superior."

"Twenty-one."

"This is State Route 15, isn't it?"

"Uh huh."

"So what's twenty-one?"

"Your age. I'm guessing."

"I'll be twenty-two next month. Look, you mean this isn't the way to Superior?"

"Not anymore. Used to be, though."

The driver got out of the car. She was wearing a thin, sleeveless dress. A wind picked up, blowing her yellow hair around her face. She walked to the rear of the car and looked at the attendant.

"Hey, you're a girl."

"So?"

"Nothin'. Just I've never see a girl gas jockey before."

"Now you have."

"You alone here?"

"Yeah, my Uncle Ike owns this station. He's sick today."

"The president?"

"Yeah, of the Black Fork Elks."

"Bad heart?"

"Uh huh. How'd you know?"

"How old are you?"

"Eighteen. Nineteen next month."

"What day?"

"The fourteenth. You?"

"Me?"

"Your birthday. It's next month, too, you said."

"The fourteenth."

"That's pretty cool, I think. Our birthday is the same."

"I'm older, though."

"Only three years."

The attendant removed the hose nozzle from the car and replaced it on the pump. She reattached the gas cap, then moved closer to the driver and extended her right hand.

"My name is Amelia."

The driver hesitated, then shook Amelia's hand.

"Terry."

Amelia took off her cap, allowing her abundant black hair to drop to her shoulders.

"You have gorgeous hair."

"Thanks. I ought to cut it. Gets in the way when I'm workin' on engines. Do you want to come inside and have a drink? Or maybe I'll bring some out. What flavor would you like? My favorite's grape."

"Orange, please."

Amelia went inside and Terry wandered over to the front of the station office and sat down in one of two adjacent flamingo chairs. Amelia came out, handed Terry a bottle of orange soda pop and sat down in the other chair, holding her bottle of grape pop.

"What's in Superior?"

"My boyfriend."

"That his car?"

"Yes. He left it with me up in Pigeon River."

"That where you're from?"

"My parents have a house there. I live in Blackhawk City."

"I've never been in Blackhawk City. I was in Pigeon River once, though. As a child. Don't hardly remember much, except for the falls. My brother, Priam, and I walked across the falls on a skinny, shaky little wooden bridge. Both ways. I was seven."

"Your brother's name is Priam?"

"Uh huh. His nickname was Tick."

"Was?"

"Maybe it still is, I don't know. He disappeared on us six years ago, when he turned twenty-one."

"Disappeared? You mean you don't know where he is?"

Amelia took a long swig from her bottle.

"Haven't seen or heard from him since. Bet he doesn't know our folks died, either."

"I'm sorry. How did they die? If you don't mind my asking."

"Plane crash. They were flying down from Huron to Black Fork in Daddy's boss's Cessna. Mr. Herbert. He was flyin'—Mr. Herbert, that is—and there was a violent thunderstorm. A big red ball of lightning struck the plane. That's what a farmer said who saw it happen. Said there was a loud bang, like a rifle shot, as a fireball collided with the Cessna. Broke the damn plane apart, my mother and father and Mr. Herbert, too. They all of 'em rained down from the sky in pieces."

"My boyfriend?"

"What about him?"

"His name is Priam. His real name. Everyone calls him Pete. Pete Farnsworth."

Amelia dropped her bottle onto the ground. The soda pop spilled out.

"That's my name. Farnsworth. There can't be another Priam. It was our mother's grandfather's name. How old is he?"

"Twenty-seven."

"Does his left eye wander?"

Terry nodded.

"I don't believe this," she said.

"He in Superior?"

"Yes. We're going to drive together to Black Hawk City. Pete had some business there, Superior."

"What does he do?"

"He sells paper products."

Amelia was crying. Terry leaned over to comfort her, putting her bottle on the ground.

"Tick and Uncle Ike were really close when Tick was a boy. He was closer with Uncle Ike than with our dad."

"We can call him, Amelia. Priam, I mean. Do you have a telephone here?"

"What for? I guess he didn't want anything more to do with us."

Amelia stopped crying.

"Look," she said, "don't tell him you met me, okay?"

"But your parents—he'll want to know what happened to them."

"No, probably not. Not about any of us. I'll tell Uncle Ike, that's all."

"Why would Pete—Priam—Tick—run off like that?"

"What's he told you about his family?"

"That he was an only child. That his parents are dead."

"He won't be lying now."

"Amelia, come with me to Superior. I'm sure your brother will want to see you."

Amelia stood up.

"You must've been a lot of places," she said. "I mean, travelin' around."

"Not so much before I met your brother. He travels quite a bit for business, and I go along sometimes. How did he get that nickname, Tick?"

"I always knew him as that. It was from before I was born. Uncle Ike played a game with him when he was little, to teach Tick how to tell time. I don't know exactly how it worked, but Uncle Ike would point at a clock and look at my brother and Priam would say, 'Tick!' Then Uncle Ike would say, 'Tock!' And Priam would say, 'Six o'clock!' Or whatever time it was. Anyway, after that everyone just called him Tick."

"It's strange how you think you know someone, know him completely, and then discover you don't. I know people compartmentalize their lives, they keep secrets, everyone does. But this scares me a little."

"You feel betrayed, huh?"

"I don't know if betrayed is exactly the right word. I'm not sure I have the right to feel betrayed. Maybe he's got a good reason for burying all this. What about you?"

"Me?"

"Yes. Don't you feel betrayed? After all, your brother did abandon you, didn't he?"

"I suppose he did. For a while, anyway."

"Here he's been in Blackhawk City all this time and never contacted you. Closer, even, in Superior. He's driven right past this place without stopping."

"You make him sound so . . . so . . . vile. Tick was always sweet to me. He was a good brother."

"Past tense."

"The summer my friend Lolly and I were thirteen, we went swimmin' one day at Foster's Pond and it started rainin', thunderin' and lightnin'. We took off runnin' for home. A car stopped on the road and the driver offered us a lift. It was a man we didn't know, he was about fifty. Ordinarily, we never would have taken it, but being that it was pourin' down buckets and the sky was crashin' and all electric and everything, we got in. Besides, he was an old guy. I figured he couldn't be too dangerous."

Terry clucked her tongue.

"Lolly got in the front seat with him and I got in the back. He didn't say much, as I recall. We were ridin' along and all of a sudden, Lolly let out with the loudest scream I ever heard. She jumped over the back seat with me, and yelled, 'Stop this car! Stop it right now!' The old guy hit the brakes and skidded to a stop right in the road and Lolly grabbed my hand and pulled me out the rear door on her side. We ran off into the woods and hid until we were sure the car was gone."

"Did he touch her?"

"No. Lolly said she looked over and there was his big old hairy thing hangin' out of his pants."

"It could've been worse. What's it got to do with your brother?"

"What you were sayin', I think. Feelin' of bein' betrayed, or almost. Lolly and me trusted that man to give us a ride out of the storm and he made it into another thing altogether."

"Thing a girl doesn't need to think about. Girls your and Lolly's age."

"That'll be six dollars and twenty cents for the gas."

Terry stood up.

"Amelia, please."

"After a lightning ball explodes, it leaves a kind of mist. The farmer who saw Mr. Herbert's plane go down said that afterwards there was a red fog around where it happened. It wasn't rainin' except for the body parts and pieces of metal."

"Could I—"

"Six-twenty."

Terry walked to the car and took some money out of her purse, which she had left on the front seat. She brought it to Amelia.

Amelia looked at the bills and took them.

"I'll get your change."

She went into the station office. Terry waited outside. Amelia came back out and handed Terry several coins.

"Thanks for stopping."

"Look, Amelia, what can I do?"

"If you want to get to Superior, go back in the direction you came from on 15 until you hit State Road 8. That's about a mile west of Victory. Go south on 8 to Highway 12 East. Take 12 all the way to the fork. Left is Badgertown, right is Superior. If you get going, you might make it before dark."

Terry started to say something, then put the change into her purse and walked to the car. She got in, started it up and pulled around the pumps. Amelia walked over to the flamingo chairs and sat down in the one she had been sitting in before. She watched Terry drive away.

A telephone rang inside the station. Amelia got up, went inside and answered it.

"Ike's Service. Hi, Uncle Ike. How're you feeling? Did you take your pills? No, not much. A few fill-ups, that's all. I've been workin' on Oscar Wright's tranny, mostly. The Olds Holiday, right. A strange thing did happen, though. Woman in a snazzy new Sunliner stopped. No, no, just a fill-up. But she had a story about Tick. Uh huh. Twenty-two next month, the same day as mine. Yes, how do you like that. I know, sure. Said he's livin' in Blackhawk City, workin' as a paper salesman. Me, neither. Right. My thoughts exactly. I never have believed it. Daddy wasn't that way or he would have done it to me is what I think. No way we ever can. Sure. You take good care now, Uncle Ike. I'll see you in two hours, could be less. I'm gonna take another crack at that tranny. Just rest, it's good. I'll fix supper. Bye now."

Amelia hung up the telephone. She walked outside and stood next to the flamingo chairs. She put her left foot on the back of the one Terry had been sitting in and kicked it over.

2

Amelia pulled the peak of her red ballcap down farther so that the rain did not hit her directly in the face as she walked. She was almost to the Victory city limits sign, where the Trailways stopped at two forty-five every day, even Saturdays and Sundays. It was two twenty-four, according to her watch; Tick's watch, actually, the Longine's Uncle Ike had given him on his fifteenth birthday, only now it had a new black leather band Amelia had made instead of the original worn-out brown one Deacon, Tick's Catahoula, had chewed practically to tatters. Deacon had finally died four years ago, deaf and mostly toothless. Tick wouldn't know his dog was dead, though he'd no doubt assumed Deacon was gone by now. By the time Amelia arrived at the bus stop, the rain had let up a little. She had only five minutes to wait, anyway. Uncle Ike wouldn't read her note until Amelia was on the bus.

"Dear Uncle Ike," she had written, "I am off to Blackhawk City on my own to see Tick. I do not have it in my mind to be gone more than a few days. I will call you and tell you if I did or did not find him. I would have told you in person I was going but then I thought I might not go if I did. I want to have him tell me why he went and stayed without a word to you and me. That girl Terry wanted to help but something strange happened in my head while I was talking to her and my brain just sort of stopped working. I am going on a Trailways. I have 18 dollars I saved and another two from the register that I took because 20 sounded better to have than 18. The bus cost 2.50 so really I will have 17.50 when I get to Blackhawk City. Tell Oscar Wright the part did not come in yet. As soon as it does after I come back I will finish the job. Take your pills. I love you, Amelia."

The bus arrived at two forty-seven, just as the rain picked up again, coming down even harder than before. Amelia gave the driver three ones and said, "Blackhawk City." In return he gave her a shiny new half-dollar.

"Why don't they have a shelter by the side of the road," she asked, "to keep the rain and snow off the passengers?"

"Write the company a letter," the driver replied.

The bus started rolling before Amelia could find a seat. There were plenty. She was one of only three people on the bus. Amelia sat next to a window in the third row on the side opposite the driver. Both of the other passengers were seated in the rear, one in the last row and one in the row just in front of that. They were Ojibway Indians, probably going to work at the paper mill in Dart Town. One of the boys was no older than Amelia and the other one not much older.

Amelia looked out at the wet woods. The sky got really dark in a hurry. Amelia pulled Uncle Ike's green Elk's Lodge jacket closer around her and closed her eyes. Pretty soon she was asleep.

Blackhawk City did not look like Amelia thought it would—or should. She had imagined many skyscrapers and millions of people scurrying everywhere without paying attention to each other. Instead, pedestrians proceeded almost leisurely, often nodding to passersby as if they inhabited a small town where everyone knew everyone else. There were a few very tall buildings, of course, but they seemed to be concentrated in one area, and Amelia was not intimidated by their grandeur.

Walking south on Tecumseh Boulevard from the bus station, Amelia stopped and inspected shop windows, intrigued mainly by women's fashions displayed on bizarrely positioned mannequins. Amelia wondered how a woman could imagine herself in any situation standing arms akimbo, legs at inelegant, opposing angles, a baleful if not entirely morbid expression on her face. The only woman Amelia knew in Victory who looked anything close to that was Constance Trenier at the drugstore. Uncle Ike couldn't stand to look at Constance's "death mask," as he described her face, when he went in to pick up his prescriptions. Constance Trenier was only about thirty years old but her face, Amelia thought, might stop a train if the locomotive had eyes.

After an hour or more of wandering around, Amelia went into a department store and located a row of telephone booths. She folded herself into one of them and closed the door. An overhead light came on. Amelia opened a Blackhawk City directory and looked up the name Farnsworth. There were only three: Alphonse, on Door Street; Mary Annette, no address listed; and P., initial only, on Lakefront Avenue. Amelia took out a pencil and a small wirebound notebook she carried in a pocket of Uncle Ike's jacket, copied down the address for P. Farnsworth and left the booth.

It had been three weeks since Terry had driven Tick's convertible into Ike's Service. The weather was changing, getting colder day by day as late summer surrendered to autumn. The Farmers Almanac predicted an early winter and warned not to expect an Indian summer. The sun was almost gone when Amelia realized she was very hungry. She walked along Tecumseh Boulevard until she came to a diner that didn't look like the food would be expensive, entered and took a seat at the empty counter.

Amelia took off her hat and allowed her long black hair to fall loose and rest on her shoulders. She scrunched up the ball cap and tried to stuff it into her left jacket pocket, but it didn't fit. Amelia put the cap on the counter and studied the menu that was written in chalk on a blackboard fixed to the wall in front of her.

"No hats on the counter."

Amelia's view of the menu was suddenly obstructed by a coffee-colored woman with a big head of bright red hair.

"Take that cap off the counter, honey," the woman said to Amelia. "House rules. It ain't sanitary and anyway, it's bad luck."

"I thought to put a hat on a bed was bad luck," Amelia said.

"That, too," said the woman.

Amelia picked her cap up and placed it on the empty stool to her right.

"That's good, hon'. Just make sure no fat man sits on it. Lots of fat men in this town. What'll it be?"

"A ham and cheese sandwich, please, and a glass of milk."

"Want that sand grilled? I like mine grilled."

"Sure, okay."

The coffee-colored woman's name, Amelia guessed, was Lilly, because that was what was printed on the nametag pinned to her white waitress uniform above her left breast.

"I like my meat hotted up," said Lilly.

The waitress inspected Amelia more closely.

"You're a pretty girl," she said, "but too skinny. Sure you don't want the meatloaf? Comes with mashed potatoes and peas."

"No, thank you, I'll be fine."

"Sure you will, honey. Only don't make a habit of not eatin' enough."

"I'm pretty strong."

"You go to school?"

"I work in a filling station. I'm a mechanic."

Lilly laughed. "Bitty thing like you?"

"Ike's Service, up by Victory."

"That a fact? You know, I ain't never been north of Blackhawk City in my life. Oh, once I went ridin' in a drop top kit car with some wild boy far as Pearl Point, but it was night time and you don't want to know that story! Well, I'd better get your sandwich."

"And a glass of milk, please."

"Lilly don't forget. Be right back."

Other customers, mostly men, began coming in. All of them seemed to be well-acquainted with Lilly. She brought Amelia her grilled ham and cheese and glass of milk but concentrated her attention on the regulars. Amelia listened to the banter as she ate. Lilly and the men laughed a lot. The diner filled up fast and Amelia had to remove her hat from the seat next to her to make room for a tall guy wearing a dark blue overcoat and a burlap cap. Amelia put her hat on her lap. The tall man kept his on while he ate.

When she had finished, Amelia asked Lilly for her check.

"How about some pie?" Lilly said. "Banana cream or cherry."

"No, thanks," said Amelia. "What do I owe you?"

"One seventy-five."

Amelia dug out two of her dollars and handed them to the waitress. "Keep the change."

Lilly took the dollar bills from Amelia and again examined the girl.

"You have a place to go, don't you, child?"

"My brother," Amelia answered. "My brother lives here, on Lakefront Avenue. At least I think that's where he lives. I'm going to walk there now."

"What number on Lakefront?"

Amelia took out her pocket notebook, opened it and looked at the page on which she had written the address for P. Farnsworth.

"Four sixty-two."

"Know how to get there?"

"Yes. Well, not exactly."

"West two blocks, that's Lakefront. North three more. It's not far."

A man down the counter shouted for Lilly.

"Take good care, hon'," she said to Amelia, then walked away.

Amelia got off her stool, put on her red ballcap and headed out the door.

Before Amelia reached Lakefront Avenue, walking west on Menominee, rain began to fall. At the corner of Lakefront and Menominee, the wind blew so hard that she had to hold her cap on her head so as not to lose it. Amelia struggled forward against the north wind, trying not to pay attention to the rain that soaked her back and legs. When she felt water running down her back from the exposed back of her neck, Amelia let her hair down, ducked her head and half ran in the direction of 462 Lakefront.

By the time she got there, Amelia was thoroughly wet and shivering with cold. She entered the lobby and shook herself like a dog. A man and a woman, both of them middle-aged, short and stout, came out of an elevator. They stopped and stared at Amelia. The man wore thick eyeglasses and a bushy gray brown mustache. The woman's face was white with rice powder and so puffy that her eyes were barely visible; they were set deep in her head and looked to Amelia like tiny black shotgun pellets.

"Are you lost, dear?" the woman asked Amelia.

"No, ma'am. I'm here to see Mr. Farnsworth."

"Pete's still in Florida, I believe," said the man.

"He lives across the hall from us," the woman added. "His fiancée is staying here while he's away."

"Terry's taking care of the apartment, Hilda," the man said. "She doesn't stay here."

"Yes, she does, Martin. She stays quite often in the apartment."

"Is she there now?" asked Amelia.

"I haven't seen her," said the woman, "not today. Have you, Martin?"

"What?"

"Seen Terry."

"Not since five-thirty yesterday afternoon. I was coming home as she was leaving the building."

"Go up and knock on the door, dear," the woman said to Amelia. "Do you know which it is?"

"No, ma'am."

"Six C."

"Thank you," said Amelia.

"Take the elevator," said the man.

"Of course she's going to take the elevator," the woman said.

"I will, thanks."

Amelia got into the elevator. The man and woman watched her until the door closed.

On the sixth floor, Amelia found apartment C. The name P. Farnsworth was printed on a nameplate above the buzzer next to the door. Amelia pressed the button and waited. She took off her wet hat and ran the fingers of her left hand through her hair. There was no response from inside the apartment. She pressed the button again and heard it buzz. Amelia stood for a minute in the empty hallway. Someone was cooking cauliflower. She decided to go back downstairs and wait for Terry to come.

On the way down in the elevator, Amelia hoped that the man and woman she had spoken with were gone. They had been kind to her but she did not want to have to explain her mission to strangers. The man and woman seemed to Amelia to be the type of people who would want to know everything. Amelia guessed that they were husband and wife, though possibly brother and sister. They looked alike in the way that after a certain amount of time together people and their dogs resembled one another.

The lobby was empty. Amelia sat down in a plush red chair but stood up quickly. Her trousers were soaking wet and it felt awful to sit in them.

It was completely dark outside now. She stood near the door and looked out. The lobby was silent. Amelia wondered why there weren't more people coming in or going out. Tick was in Florida. What if Terry did not come back tonight? Maybe she had gone up to her parents' house in Pigeon River, or even to Florida to be with Tick.

Amelia waited. Nobody came in or went out. She sat down again, even though her pants and the back of her jacket were still damp.

"Amelia? Amelia, wake up. Why didn't you tell us you were coming?"

Amelia opened her eyes and there was Terry, her yellow hair tied back, wearing a beige raincoat.

"I fell asleep," Amelia said.

"You're soaked, " said Terry. "Let's go upstairs."

Amelia stood up and put on her hat. Terry led her to the elevator.

"Your brother is in Miami on business."

They got into the elevator. Terry pressed the button for the sixth floor.

The elevator door closed.

"I know," said Amelia, as they started going up. "The people who live across the hall from him told me."

"The Morrisons."

"I guess."

"I just came to pick up a couple of things Pete wants me to bring him. I almost waited until tomorrow morning, because of the storm. I'm glad I didn't."

The elevator stopped and the door opened.

"You're going to Miami?"

"Yes, tomorrow afternoon. I'm going to stay until Sunday, then we'll come back together."

Terry and Amelia got off the elevator and walked to apartment C. Terry took out a key and opened the door. She entered first, holding the door open for Amelia.

"You have to get out of those clothes. I'll find some pajamas for you. They'll be too big, but it's better than catching cold."

Terry disappeared into another room. Amelia looked around. The apartment was small: a living room, kitchen, bedroom and bathroom; but the view of the lake was superb. Even now with rain pouring down, Amelia could imagine how beautiful it must be during the day and at night when the sky was clear. Terry reappeared, carrying several items, which she handed to Amelia.

"Here," she said, "change into these. There's a robe, too, and cotton socks. You'll stay here tonight, of course."

"Oh, no. If Tick's not here, I shouldn't."

"Don't talk stupid. I'll stay, too. You can have the bedroom. I'll sleep on the couch."

"Terry, thanks, but you don't have to do this."

"You just go in the bathroom and towel off first. I'm going to call Pete at the hotel in Miami."

"Terry, after that day. When we met. Did you tell Tick about it?"

"Certainly, I did."

"What did he say?"

"I asked him why he hadn't stayed in touch with you and your uncle."

"Uncle Ike."

"Yes. He only said that he had his reasons and that he would tell me about it later."

"Did he? Tell you later?"

"No, Amelia, he hasn't yet. Go ahead now and change."

Amelia studied Terry's face with her big hazel eyes. Terry had ladled make-up on her cheeks to conceal an outbreak of acne or eczema.

"Don't call him," Amelia said. "I don't want Tick to know I'm here. I don't want him to know I came here at all."

Amelia turned away from Terry and went into the bathroom. She closed the door. Terry sat down on the couch in the living room and watched the rain spatter the windows. The telephone rang. Terry picked up the receiver.

"Hello? Oh, Pete, hi. I'm fine. Yes, I'm coming, but listen: Amelia's here. In the apartment. She's in the bathroom, changing clothes. I didn't, of course not. How could I? You should talk to her, don't you think? No, no, she doesn't. She asked me not to tell you. When you didn't get in touch with her, that's why. She's coming. Pete, wait."

Amelia, dressed in her brother's pajamas and robe, wearing his socks, looked at Terry holding the telephone.

"I asked you not to call."

"I didn't. He called."

Terry put down the receiver.

"You told him I was here."

"Yes."

"He didn't want to talk to me."

Terry paused for a moment before answering.

"He hung up."

Amelia sat down in a chair, holding the bundle of wet clothes on her lap.

"Amelia, I'm really sorry. I'll talk to him when I'm in Miami."

"If he didn't want to see me, there's not much you can say. I'll just go home."

"Listen, Amelia, I have an idea. Why don't you come to Miami with me?"

"Tick wouldn't like it, and anyway, I don't have enough money to go."

"I can buy your airplane ticket. I'm sure once we're there Pete will pay for everything."

"No, thanks, Terry. You're being really kind, but I can't chase after him all the way down there. I just have to let it go, even if I don't understand."

They sat without talking for several minutes, then a bolt of bead lightning galvanized the sky, startling them. A few seconds later, heavy thunder broke the silence. Amelia stood up.

"I guess I'll go to bed now. I'm very tired."

The telephone rang. Terry picked it up.

"Hello. Oh, Pete, I'm so glad you called back. Yes, she is. Hold on."

Terry held the receiver out toward Amelia.

"He wants to speak to you."

Amelia stood there for a moment, then came forward, still holding her soggy, rumpled clothes. She tucked them under one arm and took the receiver from Terry.

"Hello? Yes, I'm all right, just my pants and jacket got rained on. Terry gave me a pair of your pajamas to wear, and a robe. Yeah, I'm swimmin' in 'em."

Amelia listened for a long while.

"I wish I did. Uncle Ike, neither, really. You could, yes. Just after Terry came by my brain wouldn't let it rest, so I had to come. Left Uncle Ike a note, took the Trailways. Yes, it's a little scary. Kind of cool, though, all the stores and big buildings. People here are pretty friendly."

Amelia absentmindedly twisted her trousers with her fingers as she listened to her brother, wringing rainwater from them and spotting the carpet.

"All right, I will. Either place. I'm mostly at the station daytimes. Yes, the numbers are the same. Guess you couldn't, even if you wanted to. Uh huh. Thanks, okay. He'll be glad. I sure will. Tick? I never took it personal, you know? I am. Yes, of course, I do. Why wouldn't I? You're my brother. What? Yeah, he did, a couple years after you left. Okay, bye."

Amelia handed the receiver back to Terry. Terry put it to her ear, then hung up.

"What did he say?"

"He said he still loved us, me and Uncle Ike. That's the most important thing. And that he'll call after he comes back from Miami and fix a time to come see us."

"He explain why he left cold like he did?"

"Not exactly. Maybe he will when he comes up home."

Lightning flashed again.

"I don't care, really, if he does or not."

Thunder rumbled, rattling the windows.

"That was real close," said Amelia.

Terry stood up and walked over to her.

"Would you mind if I gave you a hug?" asked Terry.

Amelia shook her head. Terry embraced her and held Amelia tightly for several seconds. Amelia thought she might cry, but she didn't, just shivered a little. Terry released her and took the bundle of wet clothes out from under Amelia's arm.

"I'll lay these things out to dry," she said.

3

Ike sat at his desk in the office of his service station and tapped his pipe bowl against the edge of an Arabian Nights Coffee can he used as an ashtray, emptying the contents into it. He stood up and stretched. It was almost closing time, ten minutes to six. There had been few customers since he had come in today at noon, which was a good thing, Amelia having taken off right after to keep a doctor's appointment in Black Fork. She was using Ike's 1948 Ford pick-up, which did not have any headlights, so Amelia would have to drive home directly from Black Fork while there was still daylight.

Ike was worried about his niece. Every so often, Amelia would suddenly feel about to faint and have to sit down and wait a few minutes for the starry particles, as she called them, to clear out of her brain. His niece told him she saw what looked like dust motes floating in sunlight in front of her eyes. Ike had made Amelia a date with Bud Proud, the best eye doctor in Tecumseh County. If it was a problem he could not handle, Ike knew, Dr. Proud would find the right person in Blackhawk City to examine her.

Ike killed the lights, locked the office door and closed down the gas pumps. He was just as happy as not to shut the station a little early since he was anxious to know what Bud made of Amelia's condition. She had not called, so Ike guessed she was not home yet. He wanted to be at the house when she got there or soon after.

Just as Ike was opening the door to his Chevy, a car drove up to the pumps and stopped. A tall, thin young man climbed out of a blue Sunliner convertible with the top up. Ike could see right away, even in the dusk, that this was his nephew, Priam. The young man walked over to Ike and stood directly in front of him. Ike squinted his eyes and looked Priam up and down.

"Hello, boy," Ike said, and offered his right hand.

"Uncle Ike," said his nephew, "you recognized me."

They shook hands.

"Let's go inside," said Ike. "I want to telephone to your sister, tell her you're here."

"Wait. Don't call Amelia."

"Why? She took a bus to Blackhawk City to find you. Amelia'd be here now, weren't for her goin' to the doctor's this afternoon."

"She sick?"

"Well, Tick, I don't really know. Why don't you want me to phone her?"

"Because I can't stay."

"Amelia told me you talked when she was down there."

"I was in Miami."

"That you called while she was at your apartment and said you'd be comin' up to visit us."

"I thought that I could."

Tick looked away from his uncle. The hills were faded red.

"I've got a few questions for you, son."

Tick looked back at Ike.

"I'm sure you do."

"Amelia says your girl was real nice to her."

"She's not my girl any more."

"You were supposed to be married."

"Things just didn't work out."

A Peterbilt labeled Deer Rapids Fast Freight rumbled by, scattering stones and kicking up a small cloud of dust. Ike turned his head away and closed his eyes. When he reopened them and turned back, he saw Tick walking to his Sunliner. Tick got in and sat behind the wheel. He rolled down the driver's side window.

"I owe you and Amelia some answers, I know that," said Tick. "The problem is, I don't have them."

The telephone in the office rang.

"That'll be your sister."

"I hope she's all right."

"You and me both."

Ike started walking toward the office. By the time he had unlocked the door, the telephone had stopped ringing. He stood next to his desk. Tacked to the nearest wall was a black and white photograph Ike's brother, Dan, had taken of his children, Priam and Amelia, on a fishing trip to Lake Washtenaw. Priam had been fifteen then, Amelia six. Dan had died six months later. In the photograph, Priam was standing, holding a fishing rod up against his right shoulder as if it were a rifle, pointing the tip straight at the camera. His left eye was almost closed as he sighted along the rod. Amelia knelt on the ground in front of him, her head tilted to one side, looking up and back at her brother.

Ike heard what sounded like a gunshot and looked out at Tick's car. His nephew's head was resting on the steering wheel.

The telephone rang again.

4

Amelia was waiting for Terry in the Caribbean Cafe in Black Fork, sitting in a window booth with her soup. Today was Tuesday, so it was split pea. Amelia always liked that Win and Nonie Hardy had named their diner the Caribbean even though it was located deep in the American middle west in country about as far removed from the Caribbean Sea as could be. The Hardys had Scotch-taped pictures from magazines of tropical places on the walls. Nonie Hardy, who was not much of a talker, once told Amelia's Uncle Ike, who had in turn told Amelia, that she did not entertain any notion of going to the Caribbean. "Never even looked it up on a map," she said. "I don't ever want to be a foreigner anywhere."

Terry was late. It was twelve-thirty and she had told Amelia that she would meet her at twelve or twelve-fifteen. The traffic from Blackhawk City could be bad. Amelia finished her soup at twelve thirty-five and sat there. Win Hardy came over and asked her if she wanted more and Amelia said no, thank you. Win picked up the empty bowl and spoon and walked away. Five minutes later, Terry arrived. She spotted Amelia, came over and sat down across from her.

"Sorry I'm late. I went back for something."

Terry opened her purse, took out a ring and handed it to Amelia.

"It's an emerald," said Terry. "Pete gave it to me. He said it belonged to your grandmother, your mother's mother. I thought you should have it."

Amelia studied the green stone.

"What did Tick tell you before he drove up here? Did he say anything about what he intended to do?"

"No."

"What did he say?"

"He'd been complaining about the nightmares. He was afraid to go to sleep."

Amelia held her grandmother's emerald ring in the palm of her right hand. She stared at it.

"Had bad dreams, huh?"

"Off and on since I knew him. The last couple of weeks were the worst."

"Did he talk about them?"

Nonie Hardy came over.

"Can I get you something, honey?" she asked Terry.

"Just coffee, thanks."

"Sure thing. What about you, Amelia?"

"I'm good, Nonie."

After Mrs. Hardy went to get the coffee, Amelia looked directly into Terry's eyes.

"What did he tell you?" she asked.

"Pete said that in the dreams there was always a sheet pulled up over his face, so he couldn't see."

Nonie brought Terry her coffee, smiled at both of the girls and went away.

"Couldn't see? Couldn't see what?"

"Who. Couldn't see who."

Amelia closed her fist around the ring.

"He said a man."

"How did he know it was a man?"

Terry lifted the cup chin high.

"A man's voice would say, 'Be a good little bear. Be a good little bear.'"

Terry took a sip of coffee, then put down the cup.

"Amelia, Pete didn't want you to know, even if he did."

"Thanks for bringing me Grammy McCall's emerald."

Amelia opened her hand, looked at the ring, then squeezed her fingers around it again.

"How's your Uncle Ike doing? His heart."

"Doc's keepin' a close eye on him."

Terry looked out the window. The sky was moving fast.

"I don't like to drive in the rain," she said.

Amelia looked up, then out the window.

Terry took a half-dollar from her purse and put it on the table.

"You don't need me around now, Amelia."

Terry slid out of the booth and stood up. She looked at the younger girl for a moment, then left the diner.

Amelia took her grandmother's ring and slid it onto the middle finger of her left hand. Nonie Hardy came back over.

"What a pretty stone," she said. "That new?"

"It belonged to my grandmother. It's an emerald."

Amelia held her hand up so that Mrs. Hardy could study the ring more closely.

"There's a bird named an emerald," said Nonie Hardy, "a bright green hummingbird found mainly in the Caribbean."

Amelia smiled at her and said, "Well, then, I guess this is where it ought to be."

The Ciné

$\vdots \quad \vdots \quad \vdots$

On a cloudy October Saturday in 1953, when Roy was seven
years old, his father took him to see a movie at the Ciné theater on
Bukovina Avenue in Chicago, where they lived. Roy's father drove them
in his powder-blue Cadillac, bumping over cobblestones and streetcar
tracks, until he parked the car half a block away from the theater.

Roy was wearing a brown and white checked wool sweater, khaki
trousers and saddle shoes. His father wore a double-breasted blue suit
with a white silk tie. They held hands as they walked toward the Ciné.
The air was becoming colder every day now, Roy noticed, and he was
eager to get inside the theater, to be away from the wind. The Ciné sign
had a red background over which the letters curved vertically in yellow
neon. They snaked into one another like reticulate pythons threaded
through branches of a thick-trunked Cambodian bo tree. The marquee
advertised the movie they were going to see, *King of the Khyber Rifles*,
starring Tyrone Power as King, a half-caste British officer command-
ing Indian cavalry riding against Afghan and other insurgents. "Tyrone
Cupcake," Roy's father called him, but Roy did not know why.

Roy and his father entered the Ciné lobby and headed for the
concession stand, where Roy's father bought Roy buttered popcorn,
a Holloway All-Day sucker and a Dad's root beer. Inside the cinema,

they chose seats fairly close to the screen on the right-hand side. The audience was composed mostly of kids, many of whom ran up and down the aisles even during the show, shouting and laughing, falling and spilling popcorn and drinks.

The movie began soon after Roy and his father were in their seats, and as Tyrone Power was reviewing his mounted troops, Roy's father whispered to his son, "The Afghans were making money off the opium trade even back then."

"What's opium, Dad?" asked Roy.

"Hop made from poppies. The Afghans grow and sell them to dope dealers in other countries. Opium makes people very sick."

"Do people eat it?"

"They can, but mostly they smoke it and dream."

"Do they have bad dreams?"

"Probably bad and good. Users get ga-ga on the pipe. Once somebody's hooked on O, he's finished as a man."

"What about women? Do they smoke it, too?"

"Sure, son. Only Orientals, though, that I know of. Sailors in Shanghai, Hong Kong, Zamboanga, get on the stem and never make it back to civilization."

"Where's Zamboanga?"

"On Mindanao, in the Philippine Islands."

"Is that a long way from India and Afghanistan?"

"Every place out there is a long way from everywhere else."

"Can't the Khyber Rifles stop the Afghans?"

"Tyrone Cupcake'll kick 'em in the pants if they don't."

Roy and his father watched Tyrone Power wrangle his minions for about twenty minutes before Roy's father whispered in Roy's ear again.

"Son, I've got to take care of something. I'll be back in a little while. Before the movie's over. Here's a dollar," he said, sticking a bill into Roy's hand, "just in case you want more popcorn."

"Dad," said Roy, "don't you want to see what happens?"

"You'll tell me later. Enjoy the movie, son. Wait for me here."

Before Roy could say anything else, his father was gone.

The movie ended and Roy's father had not returned. Roy remained in his seat while the lights were on. He had eaten the popcorn and drunk his root beer but he had not yet unwrapped the Holloway All-Day sucker. People left the theater and other people came in and took their seats. The movie began again.

Roy had to pee badly but he did not want to leave his seat in case his father came back while he was in the men's room. Roy held it until he could not any longer and then allowed a ribbon of urine to trickle down his left pantsleg into his sock and onto the floor. The chair on his left, where his father had been sitting, was empty, and an old lady seated on his right did not seem to notice that Roy had urinated. The odor was covered up by the smells of popcorn, candy and cigarettes.

Roy sat in his wet trousers and soaked left sock and shoe, watching again as Captain King exhorted his Khyber Rifles to perform heroically. This time after the film was finished Roy got up and walked out with the rest of the audience. He stood under the theater marquee and waited for his father. It felt good to be out of the close, smoky cinema now. The sky was dark, just past dusk, and the people filing into the Ciné were mostly couples on Saturday night dates.

Roy was getting hungry. He took out the Holloway All-Day, unwrapped it and took a lick. A uniformed policeman came and stood near him. Roy was not tempted to say anything about his situation to the beat cop because he remembered his father saying to him more than once, "The police are not your friends." The police officer looked once at Roy, smiled at him, then moved away.

Roy's mother was in Cincinnati, visiting her sister, Roy's aunt Theresa. Roy decided to walk to where his father had parked, to see if his powder-blue Cadillac was still there. Maybe his father had gone wherever he had gone on foot, or taken a taxi. A black and gold-trimmed Studebaker Hawk was parked where Roy's father's car had been.

Roy returned to the Ciné. The policeman who had smiled at him was standing again in front of the theater. Roy passed by without looking at the cop, licking his Holloway All-Day. His left pantsleg felt crusty but almost dry and his sock still felt soggy. The cold wind made Roy shiver and he rubbed his arms. A car horn honked. Roy turned and saw the powder-blue Caddy stopped in the street. His father was waving at him out the driver's side window.

Roy walked to and around the front of the car, opened the passenger side door and climbed in, pulling the heavy metal door closed. Roy's father started driving. Roy looked out the window at the cop standing in front of the Ciné: one of his hands rested on the butt of his holstered pistol and the other fingered grooves on the handle of his billy club as his eyes swept the street.

"Sorry I'm late, son," Roy's father said, "Took me a little longer than I thought it would. Happens sometimes. How was the movie? Did Ty Cupcake take care of business?"

The Lost Tribe

: : :

Roy looked for the tall black man whenever he walked past the yellow brick synagogue on his way to his friend Elmo's house. The man always waved to Roy and Roy waved back but they had never spoken. The man was usually sweeping the synagogue steps with a broom or emptying small trash cans into bigger ones. Seeing a black man working as a janitor was not an unusual sight, but what was unusual, to Roy, was that the man always wore a yarmulke. Roy had never before seen a black person wearing a Jewish prayer cap. Elmo was Jewish, so Roy asked him if anybody could be a Jew, even a black man.

"I don't know," said Elmo. "Maybe. Let's ask my old man."

Elmo's father, Big Sol, was a short but powerfully built man who owned a salvage business on the south side of Chicago. When Big Sol was home, he usually wore a Polish T-shirt, white boxer shorts, black socks and fuzzy house slippers. He was very hairy; large tufts of hair puffed out all over his body except from the top of his head, which was bald. Big Sol was a kind, generous man who enjoyed joking around with the neighborhood kids, to whom he frequently offered a buck or two for soda pop or ice cream.

Big Sol was sitting in his recliner watching television when Elmo and Roy approached him.

"Hey, boys, how you doin'? Come on in, I'm watchin' a movie."

Roy looked at the black and white picture. James Mason was being chased by several men on a dark, wet street.

"This James Mason," said Big Sol, "he talks like he's got too many meatballs in his mouth."

Roy remembered Elmo having told him his father had been wounded at Guadalcanal. He'd recovered and was sent back into combat but later contracted malaria, which got him medically discharged from the Marines. Elmo was named after a war buddy of Big Sol's who had not been as fortunate.

"Hey, Pop," Elmo said, "can anybody be a Jew?"

"This is America," said Big Sol. "A person can be anything he wants to be."

"How about Negroes?" said Elmo. "Can a Negro be Jewish?"

"Sammy Davis, Junior, is a Jew," Big Sol said.

"Was he born a Jew?" Elmo asked.

"What difference does it make? Sammy Davis, Junior, is the greatest entertainer in the world."

A few days later, Roy was walking past the synagogue thinking about how he had never been inside one, when he saw the black janitor wringing out a mop by the back door. The man waved and smiled. Roy went over to him.

"What's your name?" asked Roy.

"Ezra. What's yours?"

"Roy."

Ezra offered his right hand and Roy offered his. As they shook, Roy was surprised at how rough Ezra's skin was; almost abrasive, like a shark's.

"How old are you, Roy?"

"Eight. How old are you?"

"Sixty-one next Tuesday."

"How come you're wearing a Jewish prayer hat?" Roy asked.

"You got to wear one in the temple," said Ezra. "It's a holy place."

"Are you a Jew?"

"I am now."

"You weren't always?"

"Son, that's a good question. I was but I didn't know it until late in my life."

"How come?"

"Never really understood the Bible before, Roy. The original Jews were black, in Africa. I'm a descendant of the Lost Tribe of Israel."

"I've never heard of the Lost Tribe."

"You heard of Haile Selassie?"

"No, who is he?"

"Haile Selassie is the Lion of Judah. He lives in Ethiopia. Used to be called Abyssinia."

"Have you ever been there?"

Ezra shook his head. "Hope to go before I expire, though."

"How did your tribe get lost?"

"Old Pharaoh forced us to wander in the desert for thousands of years. Didn't want no Jews in Egypt. Drew down on us with six hundred chariots, but we got away when the angel of God put a pillar of cloud in front of 'em just long enough so Moses could herd us across the Red Sea, which the Lord divided then closed back up."

"Why didn't Pharaoh want the Jews in Egypt?"

Ezra bent down, looked Roy right in his eyes and said, "The Jews are the smartest people on the face of the earth. Always have been, always will be. Old Pharaoh got frightened. Hitler, too."

Roy noticed that the whites of Ezra's eyes were not white; they were mostly yellow.

"They were scared of the Jews?"

Ezra straightened back up to his full height.

"You bet they were scared," he said. "People get scared, they commence to killin'. After awhile, they get used to it, same as eatin'."

Ezra picked up his mop and bucket.

"Nice talkin' to you, Roy. You stop by again."

Ezra turned and entered the synagogue.

Walking to Elmo's house, Roy thought about Ezra's tribe wandering lost in the desert. They must have been smart, Roy decided, to have survived for so long.

Big Sol was sitting in his easy chair in the living room, drinking a Falstaff and watching the White Sox play the Tigers on TV.

"Hey, Big Roy!" he said. "How you doin'?"

"Did the Lost Tribe of Israel really wander in the desert for thousands of years?" Roy asked.

Big Sol nodded his head. "Yeah, but that was a long time ago. The Jews were tough in them days."

"Ezra, the janitor at the synagogue up the street, told me that Jews are the smartest people on the planet."

Big Sol stared seriously at the TV for several seconds. Pierce struck Kaline out on a change-up.

"Yeah, well," Big Sol said, turning to look at Roy, "he won't get no argument from me."

Johnny Across

. . .
. . .

Marcel Proust wrote, "One slowly grows indifferent to death." To one's own, perhaps, but not, Roy was discovering, to the deaths of others. Almost daily now, it seemed, certainly weekly, he heard or read of the death of someone he knew or used to know, however briefly, at some time during the course of his fifty-plus years. This, combined with the noticeable passing of various public persons who had made a particular impression upon him, had begun to affect him in a way he could not have predicted. What disturbed Roy most, of course, were the deaths of people he cared for or upon whom he looked favorably. The others—former adversaries, political despots or murderers languishing behind bars—had been as good as dead to him already. Early on in Roy's life he had developed a facility for excising certain people from his consciousness. He simply ceased to care about those individuals he felt were unworthy of his friendship and trust. He really did not care if they lived or died; what they did or did not do concerned him not at all.

During the winters when Roy attended grammar school in Chicago, the boys played a game called Johnny Across Tackle. Often upwards of thirty kids aged nine to thirteen would gather in the gravel schoolyard, which was covered with snow, during recess or lunch break or after classes were over, and decide who would be the first designated tackler.

The rest of the boys would line up against the brick wall of the school building, a dirty brown edifice undoubtedly modeled after the factories of Victorian England, which was perhaps fifty feet long. This would be the width of the field. Sixty yards or so across the schoolyard was a chain link fence. The object was to run from the wall to the fence and back again as many times as possible without being tackled. The wall and the fence were "safe." Nobody could be tackled if they were touching with some part of their body—usually a hand, sometimes as little as a toe—the wall or the fence.

Somebody would volunteer to be "it," the first designated tackler. The object, of course, was to be the last man standing. They mostly played when there was a thick layer of snow over the gravel, to protect them from being cut by the stones. Even so, boys would be bruised and battered during this game; broken arms, wrists, ankles and fingers and the occasional broken leg were not uncommon. Girls would play a tag version of the same game, a more sensible exercise. Roy thought he should have taken this as an early sign that women were, if not superior, the more sensible sex.

The boy who was "it" would survey the lineup, pick out his quarry— usually one of the weaker kids, an easy target—and shout, "Johnny Across!" All of the Johnnys would then take off for the opposite safety of the fence. Each participant wanted to be the last survivor, the "winner," except that whoever won knew he would be piled on by however many of the tacklers as possible.

If the last boy was well-liked, the others would take him down tenderly, with respect for his toughness and athleticism. If, however, "Lonely Johnny," as Crazy Jimmy K., an older friend of Roy's who claimed to have achieved that distinction more than twenty times, called him, was unpopular with the majority of the rest of the players, the result could be decidedly ugly. Often, in order to avoid an animalistic conclusion, a kid who knew he was going to get it if he managed to make it through to the end would go down on purpose early in the game and get in his licks on the tackles.

When Roy was eleven years old, he was troubled by frequent nose-bleeds. As his doctor explained, this was a not uncommon occurrence during rapid growth spurts. Blood vessels in Roy's nose would burst at any time, even when he wasn't exerting himself. One weekday morning in the middle of February, Roy went to the doctor's office to have his nose cauterized. The doctor inserted what looked to Roy like a soldering iron up each of his nostrils and burned the ends of the broken blood vessels. He then lubricated Roy's nasal passages, packed them with gauze, and instructed him to avoid contact sports for ten days. He handed Roy a tube of Vaseline and said he should not let his nostrils dry out, not blow his nose, and not pick at the scabs that would form, even if they itched. Then Roy took a bus to school.

Just as he arrived, the guys were gathering in the schoolyard to begin a game of Johnny Across. Roy ran over and joined them. The first designated tackler had already been chosen, Large Jensen, a Swedish kid who volunteered to start at tackle almost every time he played. Large, whose real name was Lars, was, at six feet tall and two hundred pounds, the biggest twelve year old on the Northwest side of the city. At least none of the kids at Roy's school had heard of or encountered anyone able to dispute this claim. Large said he had recently run into a kid at Eugene Field Park who was an inch taller and almost as heavy, but that kid was already thirteen, which Large would not be until June. Large's mother, whom the boys called Mrs. Large, had the widest hands Roy had ever seen on a woman. He was sure she could hold two basketballs in each one if she tried. Mrs. Large was wide all over but not very tall. Large's father—Mr. Large—was six foot six and probably weighed around 350. He worked over in Whiting or Gary, Indiana, for U.S. Steel. Large told the boys that as soon as he was sixteen he was going to quit school and go to work for U.S. Steel, too. His father already had a silver lunchbox with LARS stenciled on it in black block letters, just like his own, which was labeled OLAF.

Roy kept to the edges of the field, holding his head steady as he could and running at moderate speed. For some reason Roy thought that if he ran fast the intensity might disrupt the healing process. For a while,

he was able to avoid any serious contact, and in particular kept away
from Large Jensen and his mob. When Roy found himself one of only
twelve remaining boys, he knew he had to either allow himself to be
brought down without a struggle or risk serious damage.

On the next across, two of the tacklers, Thomas Palmer and Don
Repulski, targeted Roy. Palmer was cross-eyed and couldn't tackle
worth a damn. A straight arm would fend him off. Repulski worried
Roy, however. He was bigger than Roy, six months older, a little fat
but strong. Roy was faster, so he knew he had to make a good fake and
hope Repulski would go for it, then Roy could beat both of them to
the wall.

The rule was that the tacklers yelled "Johnny Across" three times. If
a kid didn't move off the safe—the fence or the wall—after three calls,
he was automatically caught. Roy waited through two calls, then, just
as Palmer and Repulski started to shout "Johnny Across!" for the last
time, he broke to his left, toward the eastern boundary of the schoolyard. This gave him more room to maneuver and would, perhaps, even
enable him to outrun them to the boundary before he cut downfield
toward the wall.

Roy slugged Thomas Palmer right between his crossed eyes with the
flat of his right hand just as he reached the edge of the field. Palmer's
glasses flew off and he went down on his knees. Roy didn't wait to see
if he had made Palmer cry or if the busted frame had gashed his forehead. Roy had Repulski to beat, and as Roy made a hard cut his left
foot gave way on the wet snow. Roy's left knee touched the ground and
Don Repulski, unable to brake, barreled past him out of bounds. Roy
recovered his balance and hightailed it to the wall. He was safe.

Palmer was yelling his head off. He claimed that Roy had gone down
as a result of their contact. Roy's knee had hit the ground, Palmer said,
so he was caught. Palmer had an inch-long cut on the bridge of his nose
and was holding the two pieces that were his glasses. "No way!" Roy
shouted. "I hit Palmer before I made my cut. He went down and then
I turned—that's when my knee touched the snow." Repulski backed
Roy up, he'd seen what happened. He started to say something else

but then he—and everybody else—stopped talking. They were all just staring at Roy.

Roy had forgotten about his nose. He looked down and saw that the snow directly below him was turning bright red. Blood was streaming from both of his nostrils. He pulled the packet of tissues out of his coat pocket, tore it open, took a wad and jammed it up against his face. Blood soaked through the tissues in a few seconds, so he threw that wad away and made another. Slowly, the bleeding subsided. Holding a third bunch of tissues to his nose, Roy leaned back against the wall. He took out the tube of Vaseline, unscrewed the cap, squeezed ribbons of it up his nostrils and set himself for the next Johnny Across.

There were only four kids left on safe. Four against thirty. Repulski and about seven other guys stood directly in Roy's path. Palmer was not among them but Large Jensen was. At the second call, Roy took off, faked left, went right and banged against Large Jensen's stomach. Roy hit the ground hard and sat still. He glanced down without moving his head much; a few crimson drops dotted the snow. Large and the rest of the gang ran off to tackle someone else.

The school bell rang, signaling the end of the lunch break. "Who's Lonely Johnny?" Roy asked Small Eddie Small. "Nobody," he said, as he walked by. Roy got up and followed him. All four of the remaining Johnnys had been tackled before making it to the fence, the last two or three at about the same moment, so there was no winner. Repulski came trotting by and punched Roy's right shoulder. "Good game," he said. Vaseline had congealed in Roy's throat. He hawked it up and expectorated a mixture of clotted blood and petroleum jelly, then walked into the building.

What Roy didn't realize until much later was that Johnny Across had been a valuable learning experience for life—and death. This business of living and dying, Roy concluded, was just one big game of Johnny Across, with everyone scampering to avoid being tackled. Back then, though, his biggest concern was how to stop his nose from bleeding. Ten days after Roy's nostrils were cauterized, he returned to the doctor to have him remove the scabs so that Roy could resume breathing properly.

By this time Roy had swallowed enough Vaseline to have lubricated his mother's Oldsmobile for the next six months.

Roy had played Johnny Across several times during this "healing" period, and had luckily avoided direct contact involving his nose except for one sharp blow by Small Eddie Small's left elbow that engendered only a brief trickle. The guys, Roy thought, did not want to witness another vermilion snow painting, so they mostly took it easy on him. He took it easy on himself, too, but Roy knew, even then, that if he kept playing it safe, in the long run he would never become Lonely Johnny.

Forever After

: : :

Riding in a car on a highway late at night was one of Roy's greatest
pleasures. In between towns, on dark, sparsely populated roads, Roy
enjoyed imagining the lives of these isolated inhabitants, their looks,
clothes and habits. He also liked listening to the radio when his mother
or father did not feel like talking. Roy and one or the other of his parents spent a considerable amount of time traveling, mostly on the road
between Chicago, New Orleans and Miami, the three cities in which
they alternately resided.

Roy did not mind this peripatetic existence because it was the only
life he knew. When he grew up, Roy thought, he might prefer to remain
in one place for more than a couple of months at a time; but for now,
being always "on the go," as his mother phrased it, did not displease
him. Roy liked meeting new people at the hotels where they stayed,
hearing stories about these strangers' lives in Cincinnati or Houston
or Indianapolis. Roy often memorized the names of their dogs and
horses, the names of the streets on which they lived, even the numbers
on their houses. The only numbers of this nature Roy owned were
room numbers at the hotels. When someone asked him where he lived,
Roy would respond: "The Roosevelt, room 504," or "The Ambassador,
room 309," or "The Delmonico, room 406."

One night when Roy and his father were in southern Georgia, headed for Ocala, Florida, a report came over the car radio about a manhunt being conducted for a thirty-two year old Negro male named Lavern Rope. Lavern Rope, an unemployed catfish farm worker who until recently had been living in Belzoni, Mississippi, had apparently murdered his mother, then kidnapped a nun, whose car he had stolen. Most of the nun's body was found in the bathtub of a hotel room in Valdosta, not far from where Roy and his father were driving. The nun's left arm was missing, police said, and was assumed to still be in the possession of Lavern Rope, who was last reported seen leaving Vic and Flo's Forever After Drive-in, a popular Valdosta hamburger stand, just past midnight in Sister Mary Alice Gogarty's 1957 red and beige Chrysler Newport convertible.

Roy immediately went on the lookout for the stolen car, though the stretch of highway they were on was pretty lonely at three o'clock in the morning. Only one car had passed them, going the other way, in the last half hour or so, and Roy had not noticed what model it was.

"Dad," said Roy, "why would Lavern Rope keep the nun's left arm?"

"Probably thought it would make the body harder to identify," Roy's father answered. "Maybe she had a tattoo on it."

"I didn't think nuns had tattoos."

"She could have got it before she became a nun."

"He'll probably dump the arm somewhere, Dad, don't you think?"

"I guess. Don't ever get a tattoo, son. There might come a day you won't want to be recognized. It's better if you don't have any identifying marks on your body."

By the time they reached Ocala, the sun was coming up. Roy's father checked them into a hotel and when they got to their room he asked Roy if he wanted to use the bathroom.

"No, Dad, you can go first."

Roy's father laughed. "What's the matter, son? Afraid there'll be a body in the bathtub?"

"No," said Roy, "just a left arm."

While his father was in the bathroom, Roy thought about Lavern Rope cutting off Sister Mary Alice Gogarty's arm in a Valdosta hotel room. If he had used a pocket knife, it would have taken a very long time. He had probably brought along a kitchen knife from his mother's house to do the job, Roy decided.

When his father came out, Roy asked him, "Do you think the cops will find Lavern Rope?"

"Sure, they'll catch him."

"Dad?"

"Yes, son?"

"I bet they never find the nun's arm."

"Won't make much difference, will it? Come on, boy, take your clothes off. We need to sleep."

Roy undressed and got into one of the two beds. Before Roy could ask another question, his father was snoring in the other bed. Roy lay there with his eyes open for several minutes; then he realized that he needed to go to the bathroom.

Suddenly, his father stopped snoring.

"Son, you still awake?"

"Yes, Dad."

Roy's father sat up in his bed.

"It just occurred to me that a brand new red and beige Chrysler Newport convertible is a damn unusual automobile for a nun to be driving."

Rosa Blanca

: : :

Not long ago I was on an airplane flying from Los Angeles to London. Seated next to me in first class was a honey-complexioned man who looked to be in his early thirties. We introduced ourselves to each other and he asked me what I did for a living. I told him I wrote screenplays for films. That was why I was sitting in the first class section, I explained; the studio for which I was working had paid the fare.

"I don't know much about movies," he said. "I like to watch them, of course."

I asked him what business he was in.

"Art, mostly. Buying and selling. Tell me, where do you get your stories?"

"From everywhere," I said. "The news, books—sometimes I just make them up."

"I've got a story," he said.

"Most people do."

"Do you mind if I tell it to you? I think it would make a great movie."

"Go ahead," I told him. "It's a long flight."

"A young man, early twenties, is shopping in a supermarket in L.A. He is dressed slovenly, and takes items off the shelves then replaces them in the wrong categories. He loses his wallet from a back pocket. The wallet falls to the floor. He is oblivious to this and turns a corner into another aisle. A young Latina comes along and picks up the wallet. She has seen it drop out of the boy's pocket. She's very pretty, no more than eighteen years old. She hesitates for a moment, holding the wallet, then pursues the young man and gives it to him. He's a bit out of it—lack of sleep, drugs, something—but thanks her, and as she turns away he tells her to wait. He sees how pretty she is. They talk. She's from Mexico, near the border. She seems a little lost, no real destination. The boy invites her to come with him to his house. She agrees, with some prodding. Her English is fairly good. He has a slick car, a drop top. He speeds to a mansion in Beverly Hills.

"The girl's name is Rosa Blanca and she's in the United States illegally, looking for work. The boy's name is Ricky, he's a rich kid who is not working 'at the moment.' They enter a luxurious kitchen. Ricky offers Rosa Blanca a cold drink. They sit and talk. A woman's voice calls out for Ricky. It's his mother, who is bedridden. She's very ill, Ricky tells the girl, and needs almost constant care. The boy goes to her. Rosa Blanca looks around. It's obvious she has never been in a house like this before.

"Ricky administers medication to his mother, returns to Rosa Blanca. After a little while Ricky's father, Mort, comes in. Mort eyes the pretty girl. Ricky tells his father that Rosa Blanca is new in town and looking for a job. He relates the story of her finding his wallet to give evidence of her honesty. Ricky clearly has designs on this girl. Ricky suggests to his father that they hire her as a housekeeper. They already have a housekeeper, Mort answers. We can always use another, counters Ricky, especially if she doesn't cost too much. It's a big property. Mort also eyes Rosa Blanca hungrily. He agrees to give her a chance, tells her she can have a room in a vacant cottage out back. Mort goes in to see his wife, Martha. Ricky tells Rosa Blanca she can move her things in today. She says she doesn't have anything to move. She's all she's got.

"Am I boring you?" the man asked me.

"Not yet," I answered.

"Good. So Rosa Blanca moves in and is under the supervision of Katy, a middle-aged housekeeper, also from Mexico—a legal resident. Katy says as long as she does the work everything will be fine. Ricky and Rosa Blanca begin a romance. He's something of a doper ne'er-do-well but he has some humor and is good looking. Rosa Blanca is not very forthcoming to Ricky about her life in Mexico; she says only that her family is very poor, she has a brother in prison and an older sister who disappeared, probably to the Boystown brothel in Nuevo Laredo. Unbeknownst to Ricky, Mort preys upon Rosa Blanca, too. She listens to his complaint that his wife cannot take care of him any more, she's too ill. So Rosa Blanca carries on simultaneously with father and son, earning more money than she ever had before.

"Ricky hates his mother, and one day Rosa Blanca witnesses Ricky withhold Martha's medication. He's unaware that Rosa Blanca is watching. Ricky lets his mother die. Rosa Blanca is terribly upset, she doesn't know what to do. Ricky tells her now that his mother is gone, he wants to kill his father in order to inherit their fortune. He's an only child. Ricky asks Rosa Blanca to help him murder Mort. She is too shaken to respond. The police come and Ricky tells them, with his father present, that he found his mother dead. He tried to administer the medication—an injection—but it was too late. The cops seem to accept Ricky's story, given the history of Martha's illness, Mort's corroboration, etc. The medical examiner pronounces Martha dead from natural causes.

"After his wife's death, Mort is more open about his lust for Rosa Blanca. Ricky discovers his father with her and goes crazy. Now he really wants Mort dead. Later, Rosa Blanca tells Ricky that she did not want to submit to his father but was afraid she would be deported if she refused. She agrees to help Ricky kill him. Ricky takes Rosa Blanca to Las Vegas and they get married. Now she can stay in the country. Mort is furious and attacks his son. Rosa Blanca stabs Mort and he dies. Rosa Blanca tells the police that Mort tried to rape her as he had done before. There is a trial and she is found not guilty, that the homicide was justifiable, in self-defense. Ricky and Rosa Blanca are now man and wife. Ricky inherits his parents' fortune, and they continue to live in the house.

"Do you like it so far?" he asked.

"I do," I said. "Go on."

"Okay. Katy, the housekeeper, smells a rat. The rat arrives in the form of Rosa Blanca's fugitive brother, Carlos, who has broken out of jail in Mexico. Ricky asks Carlos how he found Rosa Blanca, and Carlos says he heard about the murder trial—it was well publicized. Of course he needs a place to stay and Rosa Blanca, thrilled to see her brother again, persuades Ricky to let Carlos stay. It turns out that Carlos has not been in jail in Mexico, he's been in L.A.—and he is not Rosa Blanca's brother, he's her husband. They were married in Mexico, then together crossed the border illegally. Ricky is their mark, their ticket to ride. Carlos brings some bad boys around and Ricky gets beaten up when he tries to throw them out of his house. Ricky refuses to give Rosa Blanca any more money. Carlos says it doesn't matter: she can divorce Ricky and get her share. Ricky shoots Carlos dead in front of Rosa Blanca, and tells her to get out. He'll tell the cops that Carlos was trying to rob the house. Rosa Blanca refuses to leave, telling Ricky that she'll spill everything to the cops and Ricky will go to prison for murder. Of whom? says Ricky. His mother died of natural causes; Rosa Blanca is the one who stabbed his father to death; and Carlos was an intruder, armed with a pistol. Rosa Blanca picks up Carlos's gun and shoots Ricky. Katy arrives and sees Rosa Blanca sitting alone on the couch with the gun in her hand, the bodies of Ricky and Carlos on the floor. Katy takes the gun from Rosa Blanca's hand, wipes it clean, then places it in the hand of Carlos.

"Katy goes to Rosa Blanca and holds her in her arms, comforting the girl. In Spanish, she says to Rosa Blanca: 'You and I were out shopping together. We found them like this when we got back.' Katy picks up the telephone to call the police.

"As the widow, Rosa Blanca will inherit the money now, and Katy knows Rosa Blanca will take care of her for the rest of her life."

The man stopped talking for a few moments, then looked at me and asked, "What do you think? Is that a movie?"

"It certainly could be," I said. "Where did you hear this story?"

"From my mother."

"Who told it to her?"

"Nobody. My mother is Rosa Blanca. She was pregnant when my father died."

"Your mother killed your father?"

"No, Ricky killed him. My father was Carlos."

I hesitated before asking the next question.

"Did Rosa Blanca tell you that Carlos, not Ricky, was your father?"

"I grew up thinking that I was Ricky's son, but Katy told me the truth just before she died."

"Does Rosa Blanca know that you know who your real father was?"

"No, Katy made me promise not to tell her."

Rosa Blanca's son looked out a porthole window at the clouds.

"If you make it into a movie," he said, "you can leave that part out, end it where Katy picks up the telephone to call the cops. That's a better ending, anyway, don't you think?"

African Adventure Story

. . .
. . .

Samaki's mother, father, three brothers, both grandmothers, one grandfather and several aunts, uncles and cousins had been murdered by rebel boys, children, really, fourteen and fifteen year old soldiers called Clouds of Mercy in Field Marshal Omar Fawali's Invincible Army of the All-Seeing Blind Seekers of Final Truth. Samaki, whose name in Swahili means fish, justified his baptism by swimming for his life, having run to the river at his mother's urging when she heard that the rebels had arrived on the outskirts of their village, and then swum through the crocodile-infested water, listening to shouts and rifle fire as he paddled to the opposing shore. Samaki climbed up on the eastern bank of the Ngobo, looked across and saw flames rising above what remained of the blue-green morning mist. A large crocodile that had been buried in brown mud suddenly lurched toward him, and Samaki, who was one day short of his ninth birthday, turned and bolted into the forest. He never saw his village or any member of his family again.

After weeks of wandering, stealing food to stay alive, sleeping in the bush, Samaki was taken in by an order of Polish nuns, the Sisters of Immaculate Apparel, all of whom wore only pure white robes. Three months later, relatives of one of the nuns who lived in Chicago agreed to sponsor the boy and paid for his passage to the United States. Samaki grew up in Chicago, a true African-American. He was adopted by the nun's cousin, who called him Sam Fish.

Sam later matriculated to Harvard Law School, graduated, passed the Massachusetts bar, and joined a law firm in Boston, where he worked for six years before moving to New York City. Four years later Sam ran for a seat in the U.S. Congress and won. He remained in Washington, D.C., for the rest of his life, serving two terms as a congressman, after which he was appointed to a federal judgeship, a position Sam held until his retirement at the age of seventy-eight.

He married while in Congress, fathered four children, and eventually became the grandfather of fourteen and great-grandfather of three. One day before his eighty-ninth birthday, Sam told his youngest grandson, named after him and called by the family Little Sam, that exactly eighty years before he had been forced to flee his home in Africa after his mother, father, brothers and most of his relatives had been or were about to be killed. Sam told Little Sam, who was then nine years old, about being frightened by an enormous crocodile and how he had run into a forest and wandered all alone for a very long time before he was taken in by the Sisters of Immaculate Apparel. Little Sam said to his grandfather, "You were the same age as I am now." "Almost," Sam answered. The next day, he died.

In his will, Sam bequeathed one-fourth of his estate to the African Order of the Polish Sisters of Immaculate Apparel. As it happened, this Order no longer existed, the last of the nuns having perished while attempting to aid wounded children during a tribal conflict. This nun, named Sister Saragossina, was the very one whose cousins in Chicago had adopted Samaki and raised him. Sam's family used the funds intended for the defunct African Order of the Polish Sisters of Immaculate Apparel to establish a foundation in Sam's name, the sole purpose of which was to find homes in America for African children whose lives had been similarly affected and to pay for their higher education.

The family named this endowment The Sam Fish Foundation for African Orphans. Little Sam provided the organization's original logo, a drawing of a crocodile pursuing a small black-skinned boy. Soon, however, certain members of the foundation's board deemed Little Sam's contribution politically incorrect and replaced it with bronze image of his grandfather in his later years. Little Sam protested bitterly, and he was commissioned by the board to render another crocodile, this time depicting the reptile encircling the benefactor snout to tail-tip. Thus pacified, Little Sam allowed the matter to rest.

It was this descendant of Samaki's, the one known in childhood as Little Sam, who, at the age of twenty-four, became the only member of his family to undertake an expedition to Africa and attempt to locate the village next to the Ngobo River where his grandfather had lived. Remarkably, Little Sam discovered, the territory was now ruled over by Omar Fawali's grandson, who had declared himself president. Ignored by most of the rest of the world, Salim Fawali and his Invincible Army of Heaven's Most Righteously Chosen were notorious for decapitating their enemies and feeding these heads to the river crocodiles, which were known to be the fattest in all of Central Africa. Little Sam was last seen alive, by himself, paddling a canoe down the Ngobo. Neither his body nor his canoe were ever reported found.

In the same year of Little Sam's disappearance, the Pope conferred sainthood upon Sister Saragossina of the practically forgotten African Order of the Polish Sisters of Immaculate Apparel. Samaki's remaining family members were invited to the ceremony at the Vatican in Rome. The newspaper *Corriere della Sera*, however, noted in their account of the proceedings that none of the American Judge Sam Fish's family was known to be in attendance.

Havana Moon

: : :

A NOVELLA

Prelude

Inside the Havana Moon nightclub the stage was suffused in a red glow. It was a tacky place. The bad lighting disguised the tawdriness of it. The band sounded as if it were playing under water. Cora, the club manager and hostess, drew a curtain by hand and performers appeared on the stage: a half-naked, tiny, delicate-looking man, his Eurasian face painted for extra dramatic effect, wearing a sequined turban, danced with a tall blonde woman. As they danced, she became another woman, then another, and another. The dance was erotically suggestive but somehow romantic. Eventually all four women appeared simultaneously and passed the male dancer around among them. At first he seemed to enjoy it, then increasingly became disturbed. The music matched his mood. The man attempted to escape but he could not. The women encircled him menacingly. He dropped to his knees. They closed in.

I

Well-dressed people entered the front hall of a large, beautiful house. Their coats were taken, and they were greeted by either the host—Mark—or the hostess—Constance. Raymond entered. He searched the main room with his eyes, looking for someone.

"There you are!" said Robert, coming over. He inspected Raymond's person. "And all in one piece, thank God."

Raymond laughed.

"The gods, if you please. On the subcontinent, if you want to survive, you've got to be on the good side of more than one."

Mark and Constance approached the two men.

"Let me introduce you to our hosts," Robert said. "Mark and Constance, this is my friend, Raymond Dean. I've told you about him."

Mark and Raymond shook hands.

"Robert tells me you've just returned from Onfara," said Mark.

"Sierra Igual, actually."

Constance and Raymond shook hands.

"May we offer you a drink?" Constance asked.

"I'd love one. Thank you for allowing Robert to invite me. I'm in the mood for cheerful company."

"I can imagine, said Mark. "You must have seen some terrible things. Constance, I'll leave this intrepid traveler in your hands. Robert and I have to gang up on somebody. Enjoy yourself, Mr. Dean. See you later."

Mark and Robert went off together, leaving Raymond and Constance alone.

"Gang up on somebody?"

Constance giggled.

"That's what gangsters do, don't they? We'll get you that drink and I'll introduce you around. By the way, are you married?"

"No. Why? Does it matter?"

"It might matter to whom I introduce you. Come on."

Constance and Raymond were seated next to each other at the dinner table. There were twelve dinner guests altogether. As the meal progressed, Constance and Raymond were monopolizing each other, but nobody seemed to mind.

"That's one part of my life that's missing," Raymond told Constance, "not having children. I'd like to meet yours. You and Mark have two, right?"

"Yes, two girls. They're with Mark's mother at the moment. She takes them on little trips, often for days at a time. They love to travel."

"I don't always love it so much. Sometimes I wish I had a regular job, and I could just stay in one place. Then, after, say, three weeks without moving, I get restless. Maybe it's because I don't have a family, a reason to stick around."

"For some people, that's even more reason to go."

"Having the children taken off your hands gives you more time for yourself—an opportunity for you and your husband to be alone together."

Constance gave Raymond a blank look.

"Mark isn't a man with hobbies. He works hard, so that the girls' and my futures are guaranteed."

"Nobody's future is guaranteed," Raymond laughed. "Sorry, I don't mean to sound profound."

"Don't worry," said Constance, "you don't."

They laughed together. Constance fixed one of her earrings, which had come loose. Mark and Robert were sitting at the other end of the dinner table next to each other, observing Raymond and Constance. They spoke confidentially.

"You really think he'll play?" Mark asked.

"He likes Constance."

"Every man likes Constance."

"It could help us."

Mark nodded, still watching Raymond. Constance and Raymond laughed again.

"Excuse me," said Constance as she stood up, "but I've got to check up on the kitchen."

"Of course."

Constance walked off. Raymond watched her go.

A female guest sitting on Raymond's other side leaned toward him.

"I'm sure if you give the rest of us half a chance, you'll find someone almost as fascinating as Constance."

"Maybe even more fascinating," said another woman seated nearby.

"I'm sorry," said Raymond.

The women laughed.

"Don't apologize," said the first woman. "We're just giving you a hard time."

The second woman leaned over and whispered into the ear of the first woman. They both laughed.

"All right," he said to them, "fascinate me."

Later, Raymond stood near closed French doors talking to a female guest. He looked through the glass doors at the terrace and noticed Mark with two strange women in animated conversation. The two strange women were extremely menacing. Mark's discomfort with them was obvious. These women were young and leggy, like supermodels, fit and muscular. They looked like vampires and gave the appearance of possessing great strength. The first strange woman put an arm around Mark's shoulders and held him as the second strange woman kissed him violently on his mouth—a long deliberate kiss. Then the first woman released Mark and the two women departed, leaving Mark alone on the terrace. Mark did not notice Raymond watching through the glass doors.

Back inside the house, the female guest said, "Raymond . . . are you listening to me?"

Raymond returned his attention to her.

"What? Oh . . . sorry, I was distracted for a moment. Of course I am."

Raymond looked again through the glass doors but the terrace was empty. He looked around the dining room. Neither the two strange women nor Mark was there, either.

"So you've never done it, then?" said the female guest.

"I believe I'd remember if I had," Raymond said. "Excuse me for a moment."

Raymond opened the French doors and walked out onto the terrace. He looked around. He was alone. He looked up to see a full moon emerging from behind a cloud. Raymond heard a noise—it was Robert, walking out of the terrace.

The dinner guests were leaving. Constance and Mark exchanged pleasantries with them, including Raymond.

Mark said to Raymond, "Sorry we didn't have a chance to get to know each other better. I'll interrogate Constance later."

"I'm afraid I did most of the talking," said Constance.

"Well, then," Mark said, "I'll interrogate Raymond the next time we meet."

"Don't expect me to divulge all of your wife's secrets on the cheap. It's going to cost you."

"With Constance, it always does."

"Don't believe it," said Constance, "I'm glad you could come, Raymond. Are you in town for long?"

"Unfortunately not. I'm leaving again tomorrow night, but it'll be a short trip."

"Call us when you return. You have the number?"

Robert appeared. Raymond examined a framed photograph of two women dancing together that was on a side table.

"I believe I do," said Raymond. "If not, I'll get it from Robert."

"What's that?" Robert asked.

"Mark and I want to see Raymond again."

"Then you will," said Robert. "Good night, thanks for everything."

"Yes," said Raymond, "thanks for a wonderful evening."

Robert and Raymond left the house together.

2

Raymond was walking on the street the next morning when he saw Constance buying a newspaper at a kiosk. He approached her, pleased to encounter her again so soon. She did not notice him at first.

"Pardon me for saying this," he said, "but you look even better in daylight."

Constance turned and looked at him.

"Do I know you?"

"Well, ours hasn't been a lengthy acquaintance, but . . ."

Raymond realized that she was truly puzzled. She did not recognize him.

"Last night," he said, "your dinner party. I'm Robert's friend."

"Oh, I see. You've mistaken me for my sister, Constance. It happens sometimes."

"Your sister?"

"Yes, we're twins. Not identical, but almost. I'm Olivia."

"You're really not joking."

"No."

"Forgive me. I honestly thought . . ."

"And you are?"

"My name is Raymond, Raymond Dean."

Olivia offered her hand and Raymond shook it.

"I didn't mean to be rude," Olivia said.

"Neither did I. May I make it up to you? Buy you a coffee?"

She looked at her watch.

"All right."

Raymond and Olivia sat at a table in an old café.

"Amazing," she said, "I've never even seen this place before."

"I stay at the Hotel Ambassador, just around the corner," Raymond said, "The concierge told me about it the first day I was there. I come here every morning when I'm in town."

"And how often is that?"

"I'm pretty much based here now, though I'm on the road a lot. In fact, I'm leaving tonight for a few days. How about you?"

"I'm not planning on going anywhere at the moment. Are you a salesman?"

"No, I'm a kind of business scout. I look for companies to buy or invest in."

"Is it exciting?"

"Sometimes."

"Perhaps you're a spy," said Olivia. "There still are spies, aren't there?"

"I think so. And you?"

"I'm a thief."

"*That* sounds glamorous."

"I steal old images, photographs from magazines or postcards, enlarge them and paint on the image."

"Do your paintings sell?"

"Commerce is all that interests you?"

"It's what I know. But it's not the only thing that interests me."

"Let's leave the rest for our next conversation, shall we? I have to go."

Olivia took out a pen and notebook, wrote something, then tore out a piece of paper and handed it to Raymond.

"Would you call me," she said, "when you return from wherever it is you're going?"

"Constance didn't tell me about you."

Olivia and Raymond both stood up.

"Why would she?"

"I'll call you."

"*Buon viaggio.*"

Olivia walked out of the café. Raymond paid the check.

3

Raymond was walking in a corridor of a train as it streaked through the night. A very fat woman squeezed past him holding a small bulldog. The bulldog tried to bite Raymond, who managed to barely avoid being bitten.

"Not him, George," said the woman to her dog.

Raymond spotted something on the floor, bent down and picked it up. It was a postcard, dirty from people having stepped on it. On one side of the card was a photograph of a full moon over the Malecón in Havana, Cuba–an almost-platinum moon against an almost black Caribbean sky. Raymond turned it over. There was a message and an address and a cancelled postmark. The card had been mailed, delivered and received. Someone had been carrying it around and either discarded or dropped it by accident on the floor of the train. He read aloud what was written on the postcard.

"I was there. Where were you? C., Apartment 8, Via Nina, 48, Portovero."

Raymond turned the card over and looked again at the photograph on the front before putting it into one of his coat pockets. He resumed walking toward the next car.

Raymond entered a fancy hotel; the lobby was filled with well-dressed people. He walked briskly into a luxurious lounge and saw a bejeweled woman sitting alone at a table, sipping a martini. The maitre d' approached Raymond.

"May I be of assistance, sir?"

"I'm meeting Madame Luneau," said Raymond,

"Certainly, sir," said the maitre d', "she's expecting you."

Raymond walked to the bejeweled woman's table and stopped in front of it. She looked up at him.

"Jesus, Ray, I thought you weren't coming."

Raymond kissed her on both cheeks, then sat down.

"You're the last person I'd ever want to disappoint," he said.

A tall waiter wearing a tuxedo appeared at their table.

"May I bring you a drink, sir?" he asked.

"Yes, thanks. A Bombay Sapphire martini, very dry, with two olives, please."

"And for Madame?"

"I'm fine for now," said Amelie Luneau.

The waiter walked away.

"So, Amelie," said Raymond, "you're a free woman again."

"I've always been a free woman, you know that."

Amelie took one of Raymond's hands in hers.

"And I've always liked you, Raymond. I hope you believe me."

"I'm pleased to hear it."

"Don't betray yourself, Ray. He'll try to force you."

"I only work for him, Amelie. He doesn't own me."

"He thinks he does, Raymond."

The waiter returned with Raymond's martini. He placed it on the table as Amelie released Raymond's hand.

"Will there be anything else?" the waiter asked.

"Not now, thank you," said Amelie.

The waiter nodded and left. Before Raymond could pick up his glass, Amelie suddenly tried to stand up, then to steady herself with one hand on the table. She was obviously dizzy. Raymond stood up.

"Amelie, what's wrong?"

"I don't know. Do you . . . ?"

Amelie collapsed heavily onto the table and tumbled inelegantly to the floor. The waiter and the maitre d'hotel rushed over and knelt next to her. The waiter held Amelie's head. Her eyes were wide open and blank, staring at nothing.

"This woman is dead," said the waiter.

He and the maitre d' looked up and around.

"Where did he go?" the waiter asked.

Raymond had disappeared.

4

Mark was in the master bedroom of his and Constance's house, talking on the telephone. He was fully dressed, wearing a suit and tie.

"Dean is a spy for Simonetti, I'm sure of it," Mark spoke into the receiver. "Look, Robert, here's the way it is: The old man will never give me any part of the company. In fact, he might never die. Even if he does—die, that is—he'll make sure that I'll never be able to take control."

"Are you sure the timing is right?" asked Robert.

"Honey, if we don't make a move on him now, I'm afraid we won't get another chance."

Mark hung up the receiver. Constance entered, wearing a nightgown, and got into the bed, turned her back to Mark, whose back was to her, and switched off a lamp next to her side of the bed. Mark sat there, sweating in his jacket and tie, the only light in the room coming from the bathroom. Suddenly, he dropped his head and buried his face in his hands. Constance turned over and gently touched Mark's back.

5

Raymond got out of bed in the middle of the night without turning on a light. He heard a load moan, so loud that it seemed as if it were coming from his own room. He stood still for a moment, waiting to hear if this sound would be repeated. Laughter was coming from the street below, followed by sounds of motorbikes being started. Young people's voices shouted to one another in an unrecognizable language. The bikes roared away. Raymond went to the window and looked out.

An old woman was walking down the middle of the street, pulling a child's wagon filled with damaged dolls, some missing arms, legs or heads. The old woman pulled the wagon around a corner, out of sight. The street was empty.

6

Raymond was looking for Olivia's building. He found it and pressed the buzzer of apartment number 8. Raymond entered as Olivia held open the front door. She closed it behind him.

"Was it fun?" Olivia asked.

"Was what fun?"

"Your trip."

Raymond looked around–definitely the apartment of a person whose intention it is to please only herself. There was nothing bourgeois about it, a real mix of period and design with an emphasis on comfort. Raymond saw an overstuffed chair he liked the looks of and motioned toward it.

"May I?"

"Please do."

Raymond sat down. Behind him on a wall was a panel of framed photographs of the same two women dancing together that Raymond noticed in the hallway of Mark and Constance's house. On the table beside him was a black statuette, a figure of a woman. He picked it up.

"It's heavy."

"Yes, it's lead. It's called Black Madonna, a piece by a French sculptor whose name I can never remember. It belonged to my grandmother."

Raymond set down the statuette.

"I have to confess, Olivia, I don't often have fun."

Olivia put ice into two glasses, then poured a clear liquid into them from a bottle. She handed one of the glasses to him.

"Drink this," she said, "you'll have fun."

"Do you like your sister?"

Olivia picked up the other glass and sat down on the floor next to the chair.

"We're not particularly close, but I don't have anything bad to say about her."

Olivia held out her glass toward Raymond.

"To the unexpected," she said.

They touched glasses.

"I wouldn't want it any other way."

They drank.

"What about her husband? How do you feel about him?"

"Mark and Constance have been married now for eleven years, and he's still a mystery to me."

"How so?"

"I don't know what my sister sees in him, other than he seems to be a good provider. I've never had a serious conversation with Mark. As I said, Constance and I don't spend much time together."

"That's not what you said. You said that you and she aren't particularly close."

"Do you think Constance is beautiful?"

"You may as well be asking me if I think you're beautiful."

Olivia stared intently at Raymond while she waited for him to answer.

"Yes, I do. I find both of you very beautiful."

"But you prefer Constance."

"What makes you say that? I hardly know her."

"Your friend Robert is a little in love with Constance."

"You know Robert?"

"We've met a few times."

"Robert isn't exactly a friend of mine. We've known each other for a while, through business, that's all."

Olivia went to the window and stared out at the sky.

"Do you like women, Raymond? Do you like women as people?"

Raymond hesitated before answering.

"I don't know anything about them."

"You're the first man I've ever met who's answered that question honestly."

"What do men usually say?"

"Most don't answer, they just laugh or say something cute."

"Do you want to go out?" Raymond asked.

"Not really. Not tonight."

They drank. Raymond put down his glass and pulled Olivia up onto his lap. She put her glass down, too.

"You and Constance, you both . . ."

"I know."

She kissed him. Raymond kissed back.

7

Mark and Robert were sitting in Mark's car on the street.

"I'm not convinced of anything," said Robert.

"You don't have to be. Leave the convincing to me, honey."

"I mean, it's not as if we're thieves."

"In the thief's world, everyone thinks like a thief. Don't forget who we're dealing with. We *have* to try to think like him. What he would do."

"Most thieves get caught."

"No, they don't. Not if their plan is sound and they stick to it."

"Stick is the right word."

"What do you mean?

"We have to stick it to him before he sticks it to us."

A man in a slouch hat, covered with filth, started to "clean" the driver's side windshield of Mark's car with a dirty rag.

"What the hell?" said Mark.

"It's a bum."

"Hey! Hey!" Mark yelled as he rolled down the driver's side window, and stuck his head out. "Cut it out! You're just smearing more dirt."

The man in the slouch hat did not stop working.

"Get him off, for Christ's sake," said Mark.

Robert got out of the car, took a couple of bills out of his pants pocket and held them out to the man.

"Here, take this and get lost."

The man refused to stop, moving over to work on the passenger side of the front windshield. Robert tried to force the man to take his money.

"Come on, take off. It's good the way . . ."

"Robert!" Mark shouted. "Get back in the car!"

"I'm just . . ."

"Get in!"

Robert shoved the bills into one of the man's coat pockets and got into the car.

"He wouldn't . . . You saw . . ."

"Shut up, honey," said Mark.

Mark and Robert drove away just as a black limousine pulled up across the street. The man wearing the slouch hat hurried across the street to the limo. The driver rolled down the driver's side window. The bum leaned toward the driver and whispered to him.

"It's them, Dino."

The bum got into the limo. The driver put the car into gear and drove away.

A car pulled up behind Mark's car and sat idling, its headlights shining into Mark's rear-view mirror.

"It's going to be complicated, Mark."

Mark took an envelope out of an inside pocket of his coat and handed it to Robert.

"Robert, money can uncomplicate a lot of things."

Robert got out of the car, walked to the other car and handed the envelope through the front passenger side window. He then walked back to Mark's car and got in. Mark drove away.

The two strange women were in their car. The woman in the front passenger seat was holding the envelope.

"How long do you think the old man will play them along?" she asked.

"Until it no longer amuses him, I guess."

"Let's hit it."

They drove away.

8

Customers sat at tables drinking and talking. Music began and the stage curtain opened. A very tall, thin man wearing an elaborate headdress appeared onstage and began singing. The two strange women were seated at one of the tables with the Eurasian dancer.

"Luis, after you give him the cash, what do you do?" asked one of the strange women.

"I wait." said Luis.

"No! You do not wait. Luis, lemme ask you: God give you a head size of a watermelon and a dick like a caterpillar. Can caterpillars think?"

"That's not a fair question," said the other woman.

"Okay," said Luis, "I don't wait. I've got to go to work now."

Luis left the table.

The singer left the stage and the music changed. A diving board on a high platform was wheeled out along with a very small tub of black liquid, which was placed below the diving board. Cora, the manager of the nightclub, came on stage and addressed the audience.

"Bienvenida to Havana Moon," said Cora, "where one never knows what time it is—or could be. You are about to witness an act we call, 'After Darkness, Que más?' starring our very own Senõr Luis!"

The stage went dark momentarily before a spotlight was trained on Luis, who stood on the diving board dressed in a tuxedo and a top hat. The audience applauded and Luis took a bow. He then took off his top hat and tossed it down to Cora, who caught it. Again she addressed the audience.

"Senõr Luis wants me to inform you that he knows he may not survive his dive into darkness. He has had a full and interesting life, he says, and he is at peace with his God."

She left the stage, the music came up, reached a crescendo, and Luis made a swan dive into the tub of black water. For a moment there was complete silence—then Luis stood up, dripping wet, in perfect shape. The audience applauded wildly. Cora came out and returned the top hat to Luis, who put it on his head. Luis took several bows as the audience continued to applaud.

"What a man!" said one of the strange women, as she clapped her hands.

"Bravo, Luis! Bravo!" shouted her companion.

Both women got up and left the club as Luis and Cora departed the stage. The curtains closed, music played. As the women walked out, they passed a table at which Raymond and Constance were sitting, drinks in front of them.

"Do you come here often?" asked Raymond.

"Robert told me about it. I'm surprised he never told you."

"Robert and I don't socialize much. We met when he was working for Asian Gulf."

"I'm glad you called me, Raymond. It was fun talking to you at our dinner party."

"Fun?"

"Did I say something wrong?"

"No, of course not. It's strange—I seem to have heard that word a lot lately."

"Raymond, you do know that you're a dangerous man, don't you?"

"Dangerous? To whom?"

"Married women like me who have both a little too much money and too much time on their hands."

"I've met Olivia."

"Who?"

"Your sister."

"I don't have a sister. Who is Olivia?"

"Don't joke with me. You and she are identical twins—or almost, as Olivia said."

"Really, Raymond, I don't know anyone named Olivia. If you've met a woman who says she's my sister, she's lying."

"Why would she lie?"

"Ask her," Constance said, and stood up. "I think I'd better leave now."

Raymond stood, too.

"Why? I didn't mean . . ."

"Thanks for the drink, Raymond."

"Wait, I'll come."

"I'm sorry, really. It's all right."

She kissed him on the cheek.

"I just feel like going," she said.

"Constance, stay."

"If I stay, you'll have to keep me."

Constance left the club. Raymond sat down at the table. A waiter came over and spoke to him.

"You need a different kind of company, sir?"

"What's that supposed to mean?"

"I wouldn't know, sir, if you don't."

"Look," said Raymond, "let me just pay the bill."

"The lady already paid it."

The waiter walked away. Raymond hesitated, then sat down again and finished his drink.

9

Dino stood leaning against a taxicab, smoking a cigarette. Cars passed on the road. He reached into the cab through the open driver's side window and stuck a Clifford Brown tape in the dash. Dino stood and smoked. Luis arrived on a bicycle. He pulled over and straddled the bike while he removed an envelope from a satchel attached to the seat. He handed the envelope to Dino, without saying a word, then rode away. Dino looked at the front of the envelope and read a name written on it in large, black block letters: RAYMOND DEAN.

Dino tossed the envelope through the cab's open window onto the front passenger seat. He smoked and listened to Clifford Brown play "Jardu" as cars passed.

10

The Havana postcard Raymond had found on the floor of the train was stuck in a corner of the mirror on a bureau in his hotel room. Olivia, nude, stood in front of the bureau looking at the postcard. She removed it from the mirror, turned it over and read aloud:

"*Luna azul sobre El Malecón.* Blue Moon over the Malecón."

In the mirror, Olivia could see the reflection of Raymond, lying on the bed.

"Why do you have this card?" she asked him. "Who is C.?"

"I found it. I don't know."

"You found it."

"Yes, on the floor of a train. I liked the picture, so I kept it."

"'I was there,'" Olivia read aloud. "'Where were you?'"

Olivia replaced the postcard in the corner of the mirror.

"Do you know what a blue moon is?"

"Not really," said Raymond.

"'Not really'? What's not real? Do you or don't you?"

"I don't."

"The second full moon in a month. It's rare."

"*Blue moon,*" Raymond sang, "*you saw me standing alone.*"

Olivia came to him on the bed and entangled herself in his arms.

"Twin moons," she said.

"*Without a dream in my heart*," he continued, "*without a love of my own.*"

"Do you sing to all of your girls?"

"Which one of you is lying, Olivia?"

"Which one?"

"You or Constance?"

"What did she tell you?"

"That she doesn't have a sister."

"Do you believe her?"

"Is this just a big lie?"

"No, it's a little one."

"A little lie can go a long way."

"Love me, Raymond. Can you love me?"

II

Constance and Olivia were sitting next to one another on a large bed. Both were fully dressed. Olivia kicked off her shoes and lay down beside Constance, who stroked Olivia's hair. Olivia extended an arm and held her sister tenderly with one hand behind Constance's head, pulling her face toward her. The two women kissed on the lips. Constance stood and took off her dress. She left her slip on and lay down next to Olivia. The sisters caressed one another.

"Tell me you won't forget," said Olivia.

"Don't worry," Constance said, "it's just for now."

Olivia allowed Constance to undress her.

Raymond woke up. It was almost dawn; a sliver of light threaded through the drawn curtains. Olivia was gone.

12

Dino drove his taxi up to the front of the Ambassador Hotel. He got out and handed an envelope to the doorman. The doorman looked at the envelope. Dino got back into the taxi and drove away.

Raymond walked up to the hotel entrance.

The doorman said, "This was delivered for you, Mr. Dean."

"Oh, hello, Phil. What?"

The doorman handed him the envelope. Raymond looked at it.

"Thank you," he said.

The doorman held open the hotel door for Raymond.

"Have a good evening, Mr. Dean."

"Thanks, Phil. You, too."

Raymond entered the hotel. In his room, Raymond opened the envelope and out fell a wad of cash. He counted the money, leaving the bills out on the bed. Raymond sat on the bed and stared at the money. He counted it a second time, looked at it again. He went to the window and looked down at the street. After a few moments, Raymond went back to the bed, gathered up the bills, and replaced them in the envelope. He put the envelope in a drawer of the bureau and covered it with clothes. He closed the drawer, then left the room.

Phil the doorman was standing at the entrance. Raymond came out of the hotel and stood next to him.

"Phil, who gave you the envelope?"

"A taxi driver, sir."

"A taxi driver?"

"Yes, sir."

"If he shows up again, and I'm not here, find out how I can get in touch with him."

Raymond took a bill out of one of his pockets and handed it to Phil. Phil took it and without looking at the denomination put it into one of his coat pockets.

"I'll do that, sir," said Phil. "Would you like me to call a taxi?"

"No, I'm going to walk."

Raymond walked off down the street.

13

Raymond and Olivia were on the bow of a ferryboat as it cruised over the moonlit water towards Portovero. They embraced and Olivia kissed Raymond. Raymond responded to the kiss but was slightly taken aback as other passengers appeared. Olivia didn't want to stop but Raymond held her off. The other passengers saw them and moved away.

"Don't you need me, Raymond?" asked Olivia. "If you don't, tell me, and I won't bother you again."

Raymond took her into his arms more forcefully. They kissed and held each other.

"Raymond, look."

They looked up at the night sky.

The moon was rising slowly from behind a mountain.

14

Raymond entered the Havana Moon nightclub and encountered Cora in the entryway.

"You've been here before," said Cora.

"Yes, once," replied Raymond.

"With a beautiful woman. Not your wife."

"I don't have a wife."

"You're a lucky man. Do you feel lucky tonight?"

Raymond laughed, "I hope so."

"Come with me."

Raymond hesitated.

Cora offered her hand to Raymond.

"Come on," she said.

Raymond took her hand and disappeared with her into the club.

Raymond was standing on the stage with Cora. The tables were more than half occupied. Cora motioned to Raymond as she addressed the audience.

"Tonight, as a special favor to me, this gentleman has agreed to participate."

She applauded Raymond and the customers followed suit.

"Look at me, Raymond. That's it."

Cora held up her right hand in front of his face. She was wearing a ring on one finger featuring a large translucent stone.

"*I took a trip on a train*," sang Cora, "*and I thought about you.*"

"What?" asked Raymond.

"You're on a train, Raymond, going home. Going home. It's late at night, the night train. Through the train window, in the darkness, you see a woman's face, the woman who is waiting for you at home. You're anxious to see her, a beautiful woman. You haven't seen her for a long time. She's yours if you want her, Raymond. Do you want her? Raymond, do you really want her?"

"Yes, I do," said Raymond.

"She wants you, Raymond."

There was a dark hallway leading to a staircase. Raymond walked up the stairs slowly. The sound of each step he took was so loud that after three or four steps he couldn't bear it. He put his hands over his ears. He continued up the stairs. At last he reached the top. There was a door with the number 8 on it. Raymond knocked on the door. The sound of his knocking was almost deafening and again he covered his ears. The door opened. A woman was inside the room, just beyond the door. It could have been Constance or perhaps Olivia. Raymond tried to enter through the door but he couldn't get in. Raymond was desperate to enter but there was no possible way for him to get in. Raymond began to cry, then to shout, then he screamed. His cries were so loud that he had to cover his own ears. The door closed. He stared at the number 8. Raymond sank to his knees.

Raymond was on the Havana Moon stage, on his knees, his hands over his ears. The audience was applauding. Olivia sat at a table near the stage. She was applauding, too. Cora helped Raymond to his feet. He removed his hands from his ears. The customers were still applauding.

"You can go now, Raymond," said Cora, "she's here."

Raymond looked up and saw Olivia.

15

Outside on the street, Raymond and Olivia walked away from the club together. A gentle breeze rippled the leaves on the trees.

"I was there. Where were you?" said Olivia.

Raymond laughed, "I don't know."

"You really don't, do you?"

"Have you ever been hypnotized, Olivia?"

"No, I'd be too frightened."

"Afraid you couldn't get back?"

"Possibly. But more afraid of suggestions. Something planted in my mind that I didn't know was there."

"Madame Cora could have done it to me. A hypnotist can make a suggestion that will take effect after the hypnotic trance is broken. At the sound of the word 'actress' I might fall on my hands and knees, bark like a dog and bite the first person I see."

"It's very dangerous."

"So are you," said Raymond.

"I haven't ordered you to bite anyone—yet."

A soft rain began to fall. Raymond and Olivia stopped walking and let the rain hit them. They embraced and kissed.

Raymond said, "I'm beginning to wonder if it really matters."

"What?"

"If you and Constance are sisters. If there's only one of you."

Olivia broke away and started walking. Raymond caught up to her.

"What's wrong?"

"Constance is married, Raymond. You can't have her."

16

Constance was driving alone on the city streets. She turned off a main boulevard down a side street and noticed a car following too closely behind her. She sped up slightly but the other car continued to tailgate. Constance turned onto another street but it was a cul-de-sac. The other car was still there, almost touching her car's rear bumper. Constance slammed on her brakes, stopped her car, and cut off the lights and ignition. The other car stopped behind her, its headlights still shining brightly, practically blinding her. She tried to decide whether to get out and confront the other driver or stay put. She saw in her rear-view mirror the other car's driver's side and passenger side doors open. She locked her doors. The car began to rock from side to side. Constance couldn't scream. She held on as best as she could to the steering wheel, the dashboard, the seats; her car felt like a boat being tossed by waves on a turbulent sea. The sound of the car's being rocked, the bending and grinding of metal and plastic, created a terrifying feeling. Constance thought that the car's windows and roof and doors would collapse and cut and crush her. As her panic grew, she tried again to scream but couldn't. Finally, the rocking stopped. Constance held tight to her steering wheel, her fingers white and trembling uncontrollably. She attempted to utter some kind of sound but her larynx was frozen, her vocal cords unable to respond. Constance could not even whisper. Her entire body, hands and head were shaking. Constance gripped the steering wheel forcefully and tried to rip it out of the floor. She looked into the rear-view mirror, which was cracked. The reflection of her face was a pool of misshapen shards.

17

Luis was alone in his living quarters, lit by candlelight, applying his stage make-up. He put on a record–Agustín Lara singing *Solamente una vez*. Luis danced in front of the mirror. While he was enraptured by the music, Cora entered without knocking. She insinuated herself seamlessly and elegantly into his arms. They danced, although it was Cora who assumed the male role in their routine.

18

Mark and Robert were sitting in the living room of Mark and Constance's house, having a drink and smoking. They heard the front door open and close. Constance entered, saw them, and stopped in the doorway to the living room. She appeared shaken and distraught.

"I didn't think we were going to see you this evening," said Mark. "Robert was about to leave."

"Hello, Robert," said Constance.

"Come have a drink with us, Constance," said Robert. "A Calvados."

"I can't, really. I'm sorry, but I just feel like going to bed."

"Don't you feel well?" asked Mark. "Do you want me to call . . ."

"I just need to rest. I'll be all right if I can sleep. We'll talk later, okay?"

"I always take the Barbados Elixir when I want to conk out," said Robert. "Would you like me to bring you one?"

"I think I'll be able to sleep without any trouble tonight. Thanks, anyway. Good night."

Constance walked away. Robert waited until he heard her bedroom door close before he spoke again.

"What do you want to do?"

"These things take time, and a certain . . . delicacy," said Mark.

"I'd feel better if we could just . . . get rid of him."

"No, I have Constance to consider."

Mark got up, walked around and stopped directly behind Robert, who was still sitting.

"Don't worry, honey," said Mark, "I always do my best by you."

"Whenever you call me honey, I get nervous."

"I prefer you when you're nervous. Calm people make *me* nervous."

Robert took a long, loud sip from his glass.

Inside Constance's bedroom, a record was playing softly, Bud Powell's *I Remember Clifford*. Constance emerged from her bathroom and got into bed. She reached over and turned off the light. She lay there with her eyes open, listening to the song. As it ended and the record stopped, she heard the front door open and close, then footsteps approaching her room. The footsteps stopped and her door opened slowly. A man was standing in her doorway in semi-darkness. A ribbon of black light emanated from the hall.

"Constance, the Barbados Elixir," whispered Robert. "I have it."

Her bedroom door closed again. She stared at it, listening to the footsteps retreating. Another door opened and closed. Constance turned on her side and closed her eyes.

The room was dark. Constance was sleeping. Again, the door opened slowly. Mark entered. He closed the door. He undressed, got into bed and began gently to caress her. Constance responded and took him into her arms.

"I need you, Constance."

"Of course, baby. Of course you do."

19

The following afternoon, Raymond and Olivia lay in bed inside Olivia's studio apartment, having just finished making love.

"Do you think I can ever be enough for you, Olivia?"

"Enough for what?"

"To keep you satisfied, so you won't ever need another man."

"It's too early to know, for either of us."

Raymond closed his eyes.

"Wake me up before it's too late."

20

A taxi pulled up to the curb outside the railway terminal and Raymond got out, carrying a small bag. He hurried into the terminal, forgetting to close the right rear door of the cab. The driver got out, came around and closed the door, then got back behind the wheel and drove away.

Raymond rushed toward the gate, looking at his watch.

He heard the announcement: "Train for Turbania, Kalars and Portovero Sud now leaving on track six. All aboard."

Raymond arrived at track six and boarded the train's first class car. The train pulled out immediately after Raymond was aboard.

Raymond entered his compartment, stowed his bag on the rack above his seat and sat down. Seated across from him was a small man who was staring at Raymond. They were the only two passengers in the compartment.

"Good evening," said Raymond.

"*Goose tarten,*" replied the small man.

"Pardon me?"

"*Yo dipansen sloat Riparzel. Gant er Portovero. Foos?*"

"Uh, yes. Portovero."

"*Sledo nos. Mono sleda.*"

The small man stretched out on the seat as he continued talking.

"*Zookis. Mono sleda.*"

He closed his eyes, then opened them and sat up again. He extended his right hand toward Raymond.

"*Nemyo Arturo,*" he said.

Raymond shook hands with him. Arturo lay down again and went to sleep. The train rattled through the night.

21

Inside the Havana Moon nightclub a man performed on stage, lip-synching a romantic tune. Luis was seated at a table, drinking a glass of wine. Cora came to him, carrying a telephone, and whispered into his ear. Cora plugged the telephone into a jack in the wall next to the table and handed the receiver to Luis. Luis continued watching the show as he spoke into the receiver.

"*Soy Luis.*"

The voice on the phone said, "I'm meeting Raimundo."

"Who is *he* meeting? You or Arturo?" asked Luis.

"He and Arturo have already met," said the voice.

"You are a wicked man," said Luis.

Luis hung up the phone, took a sip of wine and watched the finale of the show with Cora, who was now sitting at his table. When the performer finished, they both applauded. Cora reached across the table and took one of Luis's hands into her own. They gazed lovingly at each other. He tenderly touched her face with his other hand.

22

Constance was sitting at her dressing table in her bedroom, brushing out her hair. She stopped and, as she stared at her reflection in the mirror, inspecting the lines of her face, she remembered.

A well-dressed man, wearing a hat, in his mid-to-late thirties, held the hand of a young girl, his daughter, as they strolled through a beautiful park. It was very early, well before most people were even awake, just dawn. The sky threatened rain. The girl ran toward the top of one of the hills and tried to touch the clouds. When it started to rain, her father took off his hat and held it over her head. The rain stopped and another little girl appeared, coming toward them. She seemed to glide rather than walk, as if the breeze were propelling her. She was dressed oddly, exotically; perhaps she was a Gypsy. As she drew closer, they could see that she was strangely beautiful; and, in fact, she looked almost exactly like the other girl.

As this second girl came toward the girl with her father, the first girl released her father's hand and he released hers. He bowed to the new girl. She stopped and the father caressed her face with one of his hands. The father said to her, *"Sponesta tapo."* She kissed the father, then touched the other girl's face before continuing on her way. The girl and her father watched the second girl go. She looked back once, quickly, before disappearing from view. The first girl took her father's hand and they again began to walk together through the park.

Constance put down her brush on the dressing table. There was a knock at her bedroom door.

"Yes?" said Constance.

"Darling," said Mark, through the door, "are you awake?"

"Yes."

"Are you coming down?"

"I'll get dressed."

Constance rose and put on a record, Ana Gabriel singing, *Adios, Mi Chaparrita*. She stood for a moment, listening, then moved towards her closet to find some clothes.

23

The headquarters of Kalars Industries were housed in a giant Victorian office building with an ornate façade. On the top floor sat a well-furnished, dark wood-paneled, oriental-style office. The heavy brown curtains were drawn, concealing windows (if there even were any). The only light in the room came from a desk lamp. Seated in a large leather chair on one side of the desk was Raymond, holding his small bag on his lap. Seated on the other side, behind the desk, was Simonetti, the same man who, in disguise, was both the man in the slouch hat and Arturo. He was wearing dark glasses and a tuxedo. Raymond unzipped his bag and removed the envelope containing cash.

"Why didn't you tell me on the train?" he said.

"What?"

"That you were Simonetti."

"I wanted to get a look at you first," said Simonetti, as he lowered his glasses and studied Raymond closely. "Exactly how much is in there?"

"Eighty thousand dollars. I don't know where it came from."

"I'll see that it's returned to the right people."

"They never told me what they wanted me to do."

"They were waiting to see if you would keep the money."

"Should I be worried?"

"It's not always possible to control things," said Simonetti. "The Luneau woman, for example. That was very unfortunate."

"I liked Amelie."

"So did I, but you did the right thing. Better not to have been around to answer questions."

Simonetti picked off a small piece of lint from the sleeve of his tuxedo.

"These people astonish me," he continued, "really they do. At my age, I'm not so easily amused, but they amuse me. When I was younger, I played the game differently."

"I can imagine."

Simonetti stared at Raymond's envelope.

"Ray, I've had five times this amount deposited in your account. Your loyalty means everything to me."

"I appreciate it, sir," said Raymond, as he stood to leave.

"Many people have tried to derail my endeavors, Ray. None of them have succeeded. My son-in-law won't, either."

"Your son-in-law?"

"Yes, Mark. You didn't know?"

"No."

"He's not a bad fellow, really," said Simonetti. "I wouldn't have allowed Constance to marry him if he were. What Mark lacks in common sense he almost makes up for in curiosity. Do you think my daughter loves him?"

"I'm not really the one to ask."

"No, I don't suppose you are," said Simonetti.

Raymond remained standing for a moment looking at Simonetti, and then he turned and left the office.

24

Raymond was waiting for Olivia, sitting on the stairs in the lobby of her apartment building. She entered, and without speaking, together they began climbing the staircase. Between floors, Raymond touched her leg. She stopped as he put his hand under her dress and began making love to her on the stairs.

25

Mark sat with Robert inside a dark bar.

"It's no use, honey," said Mark, "he enjoys this."

"Stop it," said Robert.

"What? Stop what?"

"Calling me that. You know I don't like it."

"I made a big mistake taking you in on this. Big mistake."

"I'm holding up my end," said Robert. "What if Raymond won't help us?"

"Then it's the end, all right . . . honey."

"Do you think the old man would have us killed, too?"

"Not me," said Mark. "Not yet, anyway. But only because of Constance."

Robert trembled, becoming visibly upset.

"Jesus, Mark, it's just business!"

"Quit crying," said Mark. "Why do you think it's called a 'hostile' takeover?"

Robert looked down the bar.

"I need another whiskey."

"Calm down, Robert. Stay cool and you'll get through this. Otherwise, as my grandfather used to say, 'put an egg in your shoe and beat it.'"

Robert stared at Mark for a moment before responding.

"I wish I were like you."

"How's that?" asked Mark.

"Just stupid enough to be an optimist."

Robert motioned to the bartender.

"Have another drink, honey. A little more whiskey will do the trick."

The bartender arrived, Robert nodded and his glass was filled. He looked over at Mark and laughed.

26

Raymond was standing on the quay as the ferryboat arrived. He saw Constance on the boat as it docked. She walked off the boat toward him.

"I've missed you," said Constance.

She looked around.

"Let's walk," she said.

They walked together away from the terminal, along the waterfront. She held his arm.

"I'm afraid, Raymond. Bad things are happening."

"What bad things?"

"Mark is in trouble. I'm afraid of what he's going to do."

"To whom?"

"To himself. To me."

"He wouldn't harm you, Constance. Why would he?"

"If he thinks I've betrayed him."

Raymond stopped walking. Constance stopped. Constance stared out at the water. Raymond touched her face, turned it toward him, looked into her eyes.

"Tell me what I can do, Constance, to help you."

"You can't do anything."

Raymond tried to kiss Constance, but she wouldn't let him.

"Come with me, Constance. Take a chance."

"You don't need me."

Constance broke away from Raymond and ran into the darkness. Raymond went after her and took her by the arm. She stopped, turned and faced him.

"Stop pretending," said Raymond.

"Are you in love with me, Raymond? Is that what you're saying?"

"I want to know if it's possible."

"Possible for what?"

"To have a life together."

"Oh, Raymond. What do you want me to say?"

"Only what you mean. Otherwise it won't work between us."

Constance turned and walked away. Raymond let her go. She disappeared into the reflection of lights dancing on the water.

27

Raymond was walking to his hotel when a man approached him. Raymond stopped.

"Raymond Dean?"

"Who are you?" said Raymond.

The man took out his wallet identification and presented it to Raymond.

"Inspector Waful, Inter-Miedo Incorporated."

"What can I do for you?" said Raymond.

"You were with Amelie Luneau the night she died," said Waful.

"Just before, yes."

"Just before?"

"I didn't know she was dead when I left," said Raymond.

"Why did you leave?"

"I thought it best that I not be involved."

"Were you?"

"Was I what?" said Raymond.

"Involved."

"No."

"Did you kill her?"

"Of course not."

"Do you know who did?"

"No. Look, I'm very tired and I'd like to get to sleep."

"There are people who are very interested in the circumstances of the death of Madame Luneau."

"I see. Who?"

"That information is confidential," said Waful.

"Good night, Mr. Waful," said Raymond. "Good luck with your investigation."

Raymond began to walk away.

"One more question," said Waful.

Raymond stopped in front of the hotel entrance.

"Were you and Amelie Luneau ever lovers?"

"That information is also confidential," said Raymond.

Raymond turned away and entered the hotel.

28

Cora was administering a massage to Luis, who was lying face down on a table backstage at the Havana Moon nightclub. The room was full of mirrors on all sides, providing a variety of angles reflecting the scene. Music was playing: Agustín Lara singing *Veracruz*. Both Luis and Cora sang along with the record as Cora massaged Luis's back and shoulders. There was a knock at the door.

"*Entrée*," said Cora.

The door opened and Olivia walked in. Cora recognized her, as did Luis.

"Pardon me, Madame Cora," said Olivia, "I wanted to see you, and they told me to . . . I'm sorry."

Olivia turned to go.

"Stay," said Cora, "Luis has to prepare for his act."

Cora patted Luis on the back.

"Arise, my beauty."

Luis got up, stretched like a cat, and rolled his shoulder muscles. He grinned like a jaguar at Olivia and then addressed her.

"*Sponesta carna, chicarina. Tapo fornieles.*"

Luis left the dressing room. Cora sat down in an old leather armchair, picked up a cigarette holder with a black cigarette already in it, lit up and smoked.

"Sit, Olivia," said Cora.

Olivia took a seat.

"What did he say?" asked Olivia.

"When Luis is in different moods, he speaks different languages. Tonight he's feeling feline. He said there's blood in your face. You are hot like a furnace."

"Madame Cora, I came with the hope that you could help me. I don't know why I believe you can, but I've heard that in certain circumstances you've been able to suggest a solution."

"For whatever you may have heard, I am not responsible. But I like to listen."

"I am in love with a man who is in love with another woman."

"This is not unusual," said Cora.

"No, but what makes the situation more complicated is that the other woman is my sister."

"Are you certain?"

"Certain?"

"That he is in love with your sister."

"When we're together, he speaks about her."

"And she—what does she say about him?"

"My sister and I, we . . . we're not particularly close. She's married to a man who does terrible things. At least I think he does."

"Does she want to leave her husband?"

"She has two children, they're very young. It's difficult."

"Does this man, the one with whom you're in love, want to take your sister with her children?"

"Her husband would never allow such a thing to happen. He controls her."

"If she won't leave him, your problem is not what you think it is. How well do you know the man?"

"My sister's husband?"

"No, the one you love."

"I've been with only two men in my life."

"He's the second," said Cora.

"Yes," said Olivia.

"Stand up."

Olivia hesitated, then stood.

"Look in the mirror."

"Which one?" asked Cora.

Cora pointed with her cigarette holder.

"That one."

Olivia looked.

"Then the next," said Cora.

Olivia moved.

"And the next."

Olivia moved.

"And the next."

Olivia moved again.

"Another," said Cora.

Olivia kept moving.

"And another. Another."

Cora raised her hand.

"Stop," said Cora.

Olivia turned and looked at Cora.

"Do you recognize any of these women?" asked Cora.

"It's just me," said Olivia.

"Who are you?"

"What do you mean?"

"When you know who you are, so will he," said Cora. "That will be the end of your problem . . ."

Cora went to the door.

" . . . and his."

Cora left the room. Olivia looked at herself in one of the mirrors, turned to the next, and the next. She sat down. Tears erupted from her eyes and streamed down her cheeks.

29

A taxi was waiting, the engine running. Raymond came out of the Hotel Ambassador. The rear passenger door of the taxi opened and Raymond got in, closing the door behind him. The taxi drove off.

Dino was driving. In the back seat were Mark and Raymond.

"I'm glad you agreed to come, Raymond," said Mark. "It's time we got to know each other better. Perhaps we can figure out a way to do some business together."

"Yes. Robert's always spoken very highly of you."

"And you've made a great impression on Constance. I'm sure she'd be pleased to have you over for dinner again. Without so many people this time."

"I'd like that," said Raymond, "Where are we going?"

"A little place across the lake. Do you like music?"

"Who doesn't?"

The taxi sped away.

Inside a smoky little club, Mark and Raymond were seated at a table next to a small stage where a band was performing. The music was very loud and people were talking, laughing and arguing.

"I've never been here before," said Mark, "Robert told me about it."

They drank.

"Raymond, can you keep a secret?"

"Three can keep a secret if two are dead," said Raymond.

"I love my wife, said Mark. "I really don't believe I could live without her."

They listened for a few moments to the music.

"This is the kind of information you shouldn't keep from her," said Raymond.

The volume of the music increased. The mood in the club became more frenzied with patrons leaping up, applauding, whistling and dancing. Mark leaned over to Raymond and whispered into his ear.

"You're right, Raymond."

Robert took a drink before he continued.

"Listen, Simonetti killed Amelie Luneau. Had her killed, anyway."

"You knew Amelie?"

"Not personally, no."

"He liked Amelie," said Raymond. "Why would he have her murdered?"

"Probably because she outlived her usefulness to him. Everyone does."

Raymond stood up.

"So will you," continued Mark.

"I've got to go now."

"Stay! Have another drink."

"Next time."

Raymond left the bar.

30

Robert sat alone at a sidewalk café next to Luna Park. He glanced at his watch, looked up and around. He seemed to be waiting for someone. A waiter came to the table.

"Storm clouds over the Atlantic," said Robert.

"With lemon, sir, or without?" asked the waiter.

"With a cherry."

The waiter nodded and left.

The two strange women entered the café and sat at a table behind the one at which Robert was seated. It was unclear whether Robert saw them. The waiter brought a cocktail to Robert and headed back the other way. One of the two strange women stopped the waiter and said something to him. The three of them looked at Robert. The waiter nodded and continued on his way.

Simonetti's black limousine pulled up to the curb in front of the café. The rear passenger window lowered about one-third of the way. The waiter went to the car. An envelope was passed by a person inside the car to the waiter. The waiter took it and the window closed. The waiter turned around and walked toward Robert. Behind him, the car pulled away.

The waiter handed the envelope to Robert and walked away. Robert picked up the envelope. Written on the front was the name RAYMOND DEAN. It was the same envelope that was first delivered to Raymond.

Robert looked up to see the two strange women holding drinks, coming up on either side of him. They sat down at his table. He looked first at one, then the other. Robert put the envelope on the table. The two strange women lifted up their cocktails and sipped them through the straws. Robert lifted his glass but was too nervous to drink. His hand was shaking.

31

A man and a woman, both in late middle age, were walking among a crowd in Luna Park. Around and behind them were roller coasters, game booths, and various vendors all lit by multi-colored lights.

"Harry, look," said the woman. "Isn't that Constance?"

Harry squinted.

"I believe so, yes," he said.

"Who's that she's with?"

"Some man."

"I can see that. But who is he?"

Olivia and Raymond were standing together, looking around. Olivia did not see the woman, whose name was Ilsa, or Harry, who approached her.

"Constance!" said Ilsa. "It's so good to see you."

Olivia was momentarily stunned. Ilsa extended her right hand to Raymond.

"My name is Ilsa Diamond, and this is my husband, Harry."

Raymond shook Ilsa's hand as he introduced himself.

"Raymond Dean."

Harry extended his right hand to Raymond.

"We're old friends of Constance and Mark's," said Harry

Raymond and Harry shook hands.

Ilsa said to Olivia, "I've been meaning to call you since we got back."

"Six weeks in Polynesia," said Harry. "Glorious weather the whole time."

"How fortunate," said Raymond. "I was once stuck for a week in a hurricane on Tonga. Even the flying fish were grounded."

Harry laughed; "Even the flying fish—Ilsa, did you hear?"

"I'm so glad we ran into you, Connie," said Ilsa, "Have you heard from your sister? I wonder how her trip is going."

"Heard there was a typhoon in the South China Sea," said Harry.

"No," said Olivia, "I didn't know she'd left."

"I'll call soon, I promise," said Ilsa.

Ilsa began moving away, tugging Harry along.

"Give our best to Mark," said Harry.

"It was a pleasure to have met you, Mr. Dean," said Ilsa.

Raymond nodded. Ilsa and Harry moved off in the crowd, looking back quizzically.

Raymond watched them disappear into the crowd and then turned to Olivia.

"That must happen often," he said.

"It happened with you," said Olivia.

"But you corrected me."

"That was different. With Harry and Ilsa, I didn't see the point."

"They might think Constance has a . . . special friend. I'm sure she'll explain it to them."

"Yes, she will," said Olivia as she took Raymond's arm. "Come on, Raymond, let's find the Ferris wheel."

They moved off in the crowd together.

Raymond and Olivia sat together on the Ferris wheel as it spun. Suddenly, the Ferris wheel stopped, suspending them in their carriage high above the crowd.

"I love this feeling," said Olivia.

"What's that?" said Raymond.

"Not being anywhere."

"It doesn't disturb you to not be in control?"

"No, probably because I know it's temporary."

Raymond kissed her deeply and tenderly.

"Was that a temporary kiss?" asked Olivia.

"Only your memory can know," said Raymond.

"Kiss me again."

As they kissed, the Ferris wheel began to move.

32

Dressed in black, Constance was walking alone along the passenger deck of the ferryboat as it cut slowly through the moonlit water. She stopped and leaned against the rail. A few passengers hurried past, then ducked quickly inside, out of the cold. Constance paid no attention to them. A man in a wheelchair, covered by a heavy blanket and wearing a hat concealing most of his face, was wheeled onto the deck from inside by a steward. The steward pushed the wheelchair toward Constance and left it next to her. The man in the wheelchair reached a hand out from beneath the blanket and touched her arm. She turned to him.

"Hello, father," said Constance, "Are you warm enough?"

The man in the wheelchair looked up at her. It was Simonetti. The steward remained in attendance.

"I can stand it," said Simonetti.

"You're going to ask me about Raymond."

"I know everything I need to know about him."

"Nobody knows about anyone else," said Constance, "not really."

"Raymond is as close to an honest man as there is. Leave him alone, daughter. You can only make him unhappy."

"What happens next, then?"

"You overestimate me, my dear."

"If I do, it's your fault."

A ring of fog began to encircle the boat.

"Whenever you hear that someone has committed suicide, what is your first thought?" asked Simonetti.

"That the person was desperately unhappy and had lost the ability to survive," said Constance. She looked down into the water. "Mother was always so sad. I wish I didn't think of her in that way. I can't remember her voice."

"I can hardly recall her voice myself," said Simonetti. "It's been so many years now since she left us. After you were born, she withdrew from me entirely, from me and everything else."

"How terrible that must have been for you."

"Remember, daughter, despair is the only unforgivable sin, and it's always reaching for us."

The boat was now completely surrounded by fog.

"Look," said Simonetti, "we're approaching Portovero."

Constance looked out over the rail. There was only whiteness. Then, momentarily, through a tear in the sheet of fog, she saw the sign and glowing outline of the Havana Moon nightclub.

33

Raymond entered his hotel room at night, carrying his small bag. He switched on the lights, dropped the bag and began stripping off his clothes as he went into the bathroom. The water ran, then stopped. Raymond came out of the bathroom, wiping his face with a towel. He went over to a desk, sorted through some papers, picked up one or two and scanned them. He put them down and went to his bureau. He put the towel down on the top of the bureau, then looked at the postcard of Havana stuck in a corner of the mirror. Raymond stared at it, then removed it and carried it with him. He sat down in a chair, holding the picture. He turned the card over and read what was written on the back of it. He held the postcard in one hand, put his head back, closed his eyes, and said aloud, "I was there. Where were you?"

As Raymond drifted off to sleep, the card dropped to the floor.

34

Olivia, *dressed like a prostitute,* was walking on a dark, rainy street until she came to a corner and stood under a shop awning, out of the rain. She put one foot back against the wall, allowing her skirt to rise suggestively, and lit a cigarette. A man approached, wearing a hat to shield his head from the rain, pulled down low so that one could not see his face. He stopped in front of Olivia.

"Do you have a name?" said the man in the hat.

"It's always the same," said Olivia, "And you?"

"I do," said the man, "but don't worry, it's just for now."

She took his arm as they walked away together.

"Don't you love the rain?" said Olivia.

"I don't mind it."

"I feel safe in bad weather."

"Doesn't everyone?"

They walked into the night.

Later, inside the Havana Moon nightclub, Olivia and the man in the hat began dancing in a dark corner of the room.

"Do you always wear a hat?" asked Olivia.

"I never take it off," said the man in the hat.

"What happens if you do?"

Olivia took off his hat and tossed it to a black woman at the bar. The man in the hat was Raymond. He moved toward the bar to retrieve his hat.

"Tell her you love her," said the black woman at the bar as she passed Raymond's hat to a man in a wheelchair. Raymond chased his hat toward the man.

"Use a false name," said the man in the wheelchair as he, in turn, threw Raymond's hat to a Turkish man at a table who said, "Find another girl," and passed the hat to a short, blonde woman in a brown jumpsuit.

"She's not who she says she is," said the blonde woman.

"She's completely mad," said her lover as he grabbed the hat and tossed it to an impish boy on roller-skates. The boy circled Raymond twice and said, "She's not who you think she is."

The boy skated under the large dress of a towering Gypsy woman. She grabbed Raymond's hat and tossed it to a musician onstage, shouting, "Get out while you still can."

The musician threw Raymond's hat offstage and out the door of the club. Raymond chased his hat outside and disappeared into the heavy fog.

35

Raymond walked hurriedly, anxious to get where he was going. He saw Constance and Mark, walking toward him, holding hands. Raymond was so preoccupied with his thoughts that he almost did not recognize them.

"Raymond, hello," said Mark.

"It's good to see you," said Constance.

Mark and Raymond shook hands; then Constance and Raymond shook hands. The three of them were a bit stiff and formal and appeared slightly uncomfortable.

"We thought perhaps you were traveling," said Constance.

"No, no. Not recently," said Raymond, "I will be leaving soon, however."

"I hope not for long," said Mark, "We'd be delighted to have you over again for dinner. Wouldn't we, my love?"

"It's been too long."

"We haven't been entertaining lately," said Mark.

"Mark's been so busy," said Constance. "Because of his unpredictable schedule it's been impossible to organize anything."

"I can imagine," said Raymond.

"And you, Raymond. What have you been up to?" asked Mark, "A woman, I'll bet. That's why nobody's seen you."

Raymond looked at Constance, who smiled and clung to her husband's arm.

"A couple of women at the dinner party were very interested in you. Weren't they, Constance?"

"Women are always interested in a man of mystery," said Constance.

"Keep 'em guessing, Ray," said Mark, "Otherwise, they'll take advantage of you."

Annoyed, Constance turned to Mark.

"What does that mean?" she asked.

"Control," said Mark, "the issue is always control."

"That comes from fear," said Raymond.

"And what are you afraid of, Raymond?" asked Constance.

"Betrayal, I guess."

"Fear, betrayal, control. I can see we have a lot to talk about!" said Mark. "Constance, we'll have to have another dinner party soon."

"We'll call you," said Constance, "Are you still at the Hotel Ambassador?"

"Yes," said Raymond, "how did you know?"

"Robert must have told me."

Mark shook Raymond's hand.

"See you soon," said Mark.

Mark and Constance turned and walked on. Raymond watched them for a moment, then turned and walked in the opposite direction.

36

One of the strange women was driving along a dark street. In the back seat sat Robert and the other strange woman. The car zipped rapidly through the city streets.

"It's the way things are, Robert," said the woman sitting next to him. "Think if you were us."

"Where you're taking me, is it where Mark is?" asked Robert. "You're taking me to Mark?"

"Like she said, it's the way things are," said the driver.

"We took a chance, that's all," said Robert.

They rode for a while in silence.

Robert whispered to himself, "We took a chance."

The woman who was driving switched on the dashboard radio, which emitted loud, terrible music. The car sped through the night.

37

Onstage in the Havana Moon nightclub, Luis, dressed in a leotard, top hat and long tuxedo jacket with tails, walked a tightrope over a bed of nails. Cora stood at one end of the stage. The club was, as usual, only about half full, but those in the audience were paying close attention, except for one—Mark, who was sitting at a table alone, obviously very drunk. As Luis stepped carefully along the high wire, Mark, in a belligerent mood, shouted and laughed.

"Watch your step, honey! This act is a real nail biter!"

Mark took ice cubes out of a glass on his table, stood up and threw them one at a time at Luis, trying to knock him off balance. Cora gave a signal to several male patrons, who got up, grabbed hold of Mark and dragged him out of the club, paying no attention to his cries of protest.

"What are you doing?! I paid for my drinks! Let go of me!"

The male patrons dumped Mark, kicking and yelling, on the sidewalk, then turned and went back inside the club. He tried to get up a couple of times but fell down each time. He was too drunk to stand. Finally, Mark lay down on the ground and passed out.

38

Simonetti was seated in his wheelchair in his office. He rolled across the room to his desk and pushed a button on a panel in front of him. A telephone rang. There was a click as someone on the other end picked up.

"Hello?" said Raymond.

"It's all over, Ray," said Simonetti. "They can't touch me now. Is there something I can do for you?"

"I'm all right."

"Son, beware of the love of women; beware of that ecstasy—that slow poison."

"Sir?"

"A Russian wrote that," said Simonetti. "You aren't married, are you, Raymond?"

"No, sir."

"Don't worry, somebody always shows up. And when they don't, it's a relief."

Simonetti punched a button on the panel and the line went dead.

Raymond hung up the telephone. He was seated in a chair in his hotel room. The telephone rang again. Raymond watched as it rang several times, but he did not answer it. After the telephone stopped ringing, Raymond got up, put on his coat and left the room.

39

Robert and the strange women were hurtling down a highway at breakneck speed, the terrible music still blasting from the radio. The car made a sudden turn off the highway onto a dirt road. It bumped along the dirt road for a few moments before stopping. The driver cut the ignition and they sat for a few moments in complete silence and darkness. The strange women stared intently at Robert. He tried to open the rear door on his side but it was locked. Robert looked at the women and screamed. The women laughed horrifically.

40

Mark was lying in the street in front of the Havana Moon nightclub. A long, black limousine arrived. Dino got out from the driver's side and picked Mark up. He put Mark into the back seat and closed the door, then got back in on the driver's side. The car pulled away.

41

A telephone rang inside Olivia's apartment. Olivia, half-dressed, came in from the bedroom and picked up the receiver after the third ring. Raymond was standing in the doorway of the bedroom, fully clothed.

"Yes?" said Olivia.

She stood, listening.

42

Simonetti and the half-conscious Mark were in the back seat of Simonetti's limousine. Dino was driving. Simonetti was holding the receiver of an old-fashioned car phone. He hung it up, then began talking to Mark.

"Mark, I want to tell you about a conversation I had recently with an old friend of mine. We were talking about our families, our children, our wives, and our dreams. We spoke about the ways in which people deal with disappointment and tragedy, great and small."

As Simonetti talked, Mark slowly regained his faculties.

"He told me about an incident that took place during the last war. A man and wife and their three children were on a boat traveling from Saffron to the Palominos. Pirates boarded the ship and demanded that everyone on board hand over to them their gold and jewelry. The man told them he had no gold or jewelry, that he and his family had exchanged their valuables for passage. The pirates cut off one of his feet and threw it into the water, attracting sharks. Again the pirates asked for his gold and again he told them he had none. They threw him overboard and made his wife and children watch as the sharks tore his body apart."

By now, Mark was listening carefully to every word of Simonetti's story.

"The pirates then demanded that the wife give them her valuables. She said her husband did not lie; they had no gold or jewelry. The pirates then threw her children, all three of them, into the bloody water where they, too, were dismembered by sharks. The woman became hysterical and jumped overboard. Somehow, this woman survived, and when my friend met her she was working as a prostitute in Cambodia. She told him, now that she had given him this terrible memory she could put it into a little box and store it in a far corner of her mind and never think about it again. She would always have it with her, she said, she would know it was there, but she would not remember it any more.

"My friend told me his head was filled with little boxes, too, the difference being that he couldn't keep from opening them over and over even when he didn't want to. 'What about you?' he asked me." 'My mind', I said, 'is one big open box. The only thing I can't remember is where I put the lid.'"

Mark looked directly into his father-in-law's eyes. Simonetti lifted one of his hands and tenderly caressed Mark's face. Mark shivered visibly at Simonetti's touch. Simonetti withdrew his hand.

The car pulled up in front of Mark and Constance's house.

43

Raymond stood near a window in Olivia's apartment. Olivia appeared, fully dressed, and attached the earrings Constance was wearing at the dinner party. Raymond stared at the earrings.

"I have to leave now," said Olivia.

"Has something happened?" asked Raymond.

"Yes."

"Do you want to tell me?"

"No."

"Why are you suddenly acting so strangely?"

"Am I?"

"Olivia, what's going on?"

"I just have to go, that's all."

Raymond approached her, but she recoiled from his touch. He tried to kiss her but she turned her head away.

"Is it the children?"

"No."

They stared at one another. Olivia was about to say something more, but did not.

"I'll go with you."

"You can't. I mean, I'll be all right by myself."

"I don't like this mystery. We've never once spent an entire night together."

"I thought you enjoyed mysterious women."

"Why can't you trust me?"

"It's not a question of trust."

"What is the question, then?"

Olivia put on her coat and picked up her purse.

"You don't want me to wait for you?" said Raymond.

"I don't know what time I'll be back."

Raymond put on his coat.

"I don't know when I'll be back, either," he said.

"Goodnight, Raymond."

Olivia left the apartment, closing the door behind her. Raymond stood there, listening to Olivia's footsteps disappearing down the hall.

44

Robert and the two strange women walked on a path through a dark forest. Robert was walking a few steps ahead of them.

"I didn't think I'd be thrown to the wolves like this," said Robert.

One of the women responded, "Not exactly to the wolves."

The two strange women laughed.

"Stop there," said one of them.

Robert stopped walking, as did the women.

The woman who had been driving said, "Okay, Robert. Now!"

Robert started running. The two strange women turned toward each other and began chanting simultaneously.

"One steamboat, two steamboat, three steamboat, four steamboat, five steamboat, six steamboat, seven steamboat, eight steamboat, nine steamboat, *ten* steamboat!"

The two strange women raced after Robert, shrieking like Valkyries.

45

As Raymond exited Olivia's apartment building, he almost knocked down the old woman pulling her wagon filled with damaged dolls.

"Pardon me," said Raymond, "Sorry, I wasn't looking where I was going."

"Who does?" said the old woman as she turned away and continued on down the street.

Raymond watched her go.

At that same moment, Cora, a cigarette dangling from her lips, sat inside her office at the Havana Moon. She was counting bills, the evening's take.

"The blue moon is coming."

Cora looked into a dimly lit corner and saw Simonetti sitting in a chair.

"We have to stop meeting like this," she said.

"We stopped meeting a long time ago. Have you forgotten?"

Cora stopped counting the money and said, "My heart is not made of stone, but there is still a stone on it."

"There is a stone on mine, too," said Simonetti.

"You put them there."

"It's a custom in some cultures to place a stone on the grave of a loved one each time you visit it."

Cora looked away and resumed counting the money.

"Arthur," she said, "You're so old-fashioned."

46

Raymond was standing in front of Mark and Constance's house. He walked up the steps and rang the bell. Constance opened the door. She was dressed the same as Olivia had been moments before.

"Raymond," said Constance, "I didn't expect to see you."

"Nobody has a right to expect anything," he replied.

"I don't know about that, but I'm glad to see you. It's a nice surprise. Come in."

Raymond entered the house. Constance led him into the living room.

"Please, Raymond, make yourself comfortable."

Raymond sat down on a couch. Constance brought a bottle of wine and two glasses and set them down on a table in front of the couch. She sat down near Raymond, poured wine into the glasses and handed one to him. She raised her glass.

"What shall we drink to?" she said.

"The unexpected," said Raymond.

"To the unexpected, then."

They touched glasses and drank. Raymond put his glass down on the table and stood up.

"Did Mark tell you that he and I met? That we went to a club? Before

I encountered you with him in the park."

"No," said Constance, "are you and Mark doing business together?"

"He wanted to tell me about you."

"Me?"

"Can we stop this game now?"

"Raymond, don't."

"Why Olivia? Why lie to me?"

"Olivia, whoever she is, is the one who's lying. Ask her."

"I already did," said Raymond.

"And what did she say?"

"A little lie can go a long way."

"No, *you* said that."

Raymond moved toward Constance and stood hovering over her.

"How do you know that? Did Olivia tell you?"

Constance realized she had betrayed herself. Raymond stared at her. They heard a noise and looked over to see Mark, half-dressed, groggily approaching them. He was obviously drunk and badly hung over.

"Mark," said Constance, "I thought you were still sleeping. How do you feel?"

Mark stumbled to a chair and sat down heavily.

"How do I look? Hello, Raymond. I had a bad night—or day, or whenever it was."

"I'll make you a coffee," said Constance.

She stood up.

"I have to go," said Raymond.

"Sorry, Raymond," said Mark, "next time I'll be in better shape."

"Don't worry about it."

Constance moved toward Raymond and said, "I'll see you out."

Mark slumped down in a chair and closed his eyes. Raymond headed for the front door, followed by Constance. At the door, they stopped and faced each other.

"Olivia was right about one thing," said Raymond.

Constance looked into his eyes.

"She said I could never have you."

He started out the door.

"Raymond . . ."

He paused, looking back.

"Nobody's safe," said Constance.

Raymond left. Constance closed the door.

47

Simonetti was inside his office, seated behind his desk in his wheelchair. Standing on the other side of the desk was Inspector Waful.

"There is nothing illegal about taking out a life insurance policy on another person without their knowledge," explained Simonetti.

"That's true," said Waful.

"I take out insurance on everyone who works for me. I believe it's called a 'Peasant Policy.'"

"Yes."

"Are you a delivery boy for the insurance company?"

"What do you mean?" said Waful, "I told you that I work for Inter-Miedo."

"Do you have my check?"

"They've told me no payment will be issued until the company is satisfied that Madame Luneau died a natural death."

"Have they evidence to the contrary?"

"Not yet."

Simonetti opened a drawer in the desk and took out a gun. He held the gun to his right temple and cocked it.

"There are two bullets in this revolver."

He spun the chamber.

"Inspector Waful, let's play Russian Roulette. If I lose, Inter-Miedo can keep the benefit owed to Kalars Industries on this policy. If you lose, you'll be off the case, so it won't matter to you. If we both win, we'll cut the baby in half. How about it?"

"You're insane," said Waful. "Put that gun away."

Simonetti pulled the trigger. The chamber clicked over. He held the pistol out toward Waful.

"Come on, Inspector, the insurance business is a game. Be a sport."

Waful walked out of the office. Simonetti sat quietly for a moment. Then he lifted the revolver again to his head, cocked it, and pulled the trigger.

48

It was pitch black as the ferryboat churned through the water. Foghorns sounded warnings throughout the heavy mist. Out of the fog walked Constance. Another woman was barely discernible standing at the rail farther along the deck. Constance approached her. As she did, the other woman turned to look at her. It was Olivia. Constance stopped next to her and for a moment they stared at one another.

"Are you sure that I'm the one you've come to see?" said Olivia.

"You're the only one," said Constance.

"You didn't give him enough, Constance."

"What do you mean?"

"All you gave him was me," said Olivia.

"I didn't want to hurt Mark."

"Stop lying to yourself."

"You're the liar."

"No, I'm the lie."

Olivia moved closer to Constance and whispered in her ear.

"I love you, sister," said Olivia, as she removed a switchblade knife from her purse. She opened it and stabbed Constance in the back, then pulled it out. Constance staggered, turned around and faced Olivia, who stabbed Constance again, this time in the stomach. Constance stumbled to the rail and clung to it. The fog rolled in, surrounding the sisters.

There was a splash as someone fell overboard into the water. The fog cleared away and only Constance remained as before, holding onto the rail. Olivia was gone. The fog rolled in again, enshrouding Constance.

Constance screamed, "Olivia!"

Mark woke up. They were both lying in bed inside their house.

"What is it, baby?" said Mark. "What's wrong?"

Constance, fully awake now, realized she had been dreaming. She caressed Mark.

"Nothing," she said. "Go back to sleep. I'm all right now."

The phone rang. On the second ring, Mark picked it up.

"Hello?" said Mark, still groggy. "Oh, hi. How are you? Sure."

He passed the phone to Constance.

"It's Olivia."

49

Dino's taxi stopped at a light. The man in the slouch hat, which was pulled down over his face, suddenly appeared and began wiping the windshield with a dirty rag, smearing the grime around on the glass. Dino stuck his head out of the driver's side window.

"Cut it out," he said. "Get in."

The man in the slouch hat got into the front passenger seat of the cab. Dino stepped on the gas. The man took off his hat. It was Simonetti.

"*Escudo dos mujas,*" he said.

"You know I don't understand Kalars," said Dino.

"Your parents did."

"They never taught me. They wanted me to be a citizen of the New World."

"The Old World wasn't all bad," said Simonetti.

They rode along in silence.

50

The ferryboat moved through the fog. The clouds parted for a moment, revealing a full moon. The clouds again covered the moon.

51

The Havana Moon nightclub was empty. It was sometime late night or early morning. Onstage, Luis was sitting on a bench at a piano. He played and sang a tune:

"*I'll be seeing you / in some familiar places . . .*"

Luis stopped, picked up a cigarette and lit it with a snap of his fingers. With the cigarette hanging from his lips, he played the tune. Cora entered and caressed Luis's head.

"My love," said Cora, "tell me you'll never leave me."

"I'll never leave you."

"Everyone else can come and go."

They smiled at each other.

"What do they know about love?" said Luis.

Cora sat down next to Luis and put her head on his shoulder as he played and sang:

"*I'll be looking at the moon / And I'll be seeing you.*"

52

The two strange women arrived in their car in front of Constance and Mark's house and parked at the curb. Robert got out of the back seat and went up the steps to the house.

"There goes a changed man," said the woman who was driving.

"Men don't change," said the other strange woman, "they just forget for a little while. Then they forget what they forgot."

The women laughed. The car pulled away.

53

Mark opened his door. Robert entered, looking bedraggled and exhausted.

"I need a drink," he said.

Mark closed the front door. They went into the living room.

"I was wrong," said Mark.

"About?"

"Whiskey alone won't do it."

"Do what?" said Robert, as he poured himself a glass of whiskey.

"To be a true optimist," said Mark, "a person has to be born stupid, and be stubborn enough to stay that way."

Robert looked at Mark.

"Pour one for me, too," said Mark.

Robert made a drink for Mark and handed it to him. Mark raised his glass to Robert, who responded in kind.

"It's a bitch being just a little smart, honey, isn't it?" said Mark.

"Better to be a genius, like Simonetti."

"To the rest of us."

They touched glasses and drank.

54

Raymond was walking along the street near the harbor. He stopped across the street from Olivia's apartment house and looked up at her windows for one last time. He began walking again when he saw a taxi coming down the street. In it was Constance or Olivia—or a woman who looked remarkably like them. The taxi stopped in front of her apartment house. The driver got out, opened the trunk and took out several pieces of luggage. The woman got out—she resembled Constance/Olivia but was dressed differently than Raymond had ever seen her before. She was wearing a Chinese dress, and her hair was styled differently. Raymond watched her go upstairs with the driver carrying suitcases. He waited in the street and looked up at the apartment. Lights went on. The taxi driver came out of the building, got in his taxi and drove away. Raymond crossed the street and entered the building.

The woman was on the telephone inside her apartment. She was smoking a cigarette.

"It's good to hear your voice, too," she said into the receiver.

There was a knock at the door.

"Somebody's knocking on the door. Probably the taxi driver. I must have left something in the cab. Yes, Shanghai was fantastic. I'll tell you all about it when you get here. Right. See you soon. Mmwuh."

She hung up, went to the door, and opened it. Raymond was standing in the hallway.

"Constance," he said.

"No, my name is Olivia. Who are you?"

Raymond walked in uninvited—he was angry, deeply disturbed by what he perceived as a charade.

"You're really a sick woman!"

Olivia backed away as Raymond barged in. He kicked the door shut behind him. Her fear was palpable.

"Who are you? What do you want?" she said.

"I thought I wanted you," said Raymond, "the real you—despite your silly game."

"What game?"

"Did you really think you could fool me forever? How many others fell for it? You're lucky none of them tried to kill you. Or did they? And since when did you start smoking?"

Olivia put out her cigarette.

"I'm going to call the police if you don't get out," she said.

Raymond grabbed her arms and shook her.

"You're a bitch, Constance—a bitch and a whore!"

Olivia picked up the black statuette Raymond had admired the first time he visited the apartment. He couldn't control her, caught up as she was in her own desperate frenzy. Olivia hit Raymond in the head with the statuette. He collapsed to the floor.

Slowly, Raymond's consciousness returned. He was looking up but his vision was blurred. Two shapes were hovering over him. Eventually, his vision cleared and he saw the faces of two women looking down at him. Constance and the real Olivia. He stared at them.

The two women helped Raymond to his feet. He was a bit unsteady. He looked at each of the women, studying their faces.

"Raymond," said Constance, "the woman you're looking for is gone."

55

Raymond stood at the rail as the ferryboat glided through the water. He took the postcard that he found on the train out of his pocket, looked at it, then tossed it into the water. Moonlight shimmered on the floating postcard.

Simonetti appeared from the shadows and stood next to Raymond at the rail. Raymond did not turn to look at him.

"It's not so difficult to accept, is it, Ray? Often what appears to be contradictory or flies in the face of received opinion may in fact be true. The obvious is sadly overrated."

Simonetti placed a gloved hand on Raymond's left shoulder.

"Dear Raymond, consider yourself fortunate to have survived. I do."

Together they stared out at the water.

56

It was Sunday, around noon. Mark and Constance effusively greeted their two daughters on the front steps of their house. The two daughters and Mark entered the house. Constance lingered for a moment alone in the doorway, looking out. Then she turned, went inside, and closed the door behind her.

Holiday from Women

: : :

Bobby Newby had three women in his life, each of whom provided ingredients important if not essential to his existence. He was no longer a young man, having already passed what almost certainly had been the majority of his reasonably expected lifetime.

His ex-wife and he had raised three children, now grown to adulthood, and, following a couple of difficult years before and after the divorce, had resumed to some degree the friendship that had been the basis of their twenty-four year marriage. This friendship, Bobby knew, he would have terrible difficulty doing without, seeing as how his ex-wife was the one person in the world he trusted above all others. His devotion to her remained undiminished; nobody could ever replace her in his affections.

Bobby's former companion, the woman he had taken up with after the collapse of his marriage, still held a romantic fascination for him. She was equally irreplaceable, simply because never before meeting and living with her—for four years—had he felt so completely engaged emotionally. The problem with both of these women, Bobby had discovered, was that for various reasons he could not live happily with them, reasons that did not, he concluded after considerable contemplation, connote fault on either of their parts.

His current girlfriend, who was much younger than he, was—for the time being—more accepting of his desire to maintain separate residences, though she had recently, after dating Bobby for a year, been suggesting that, being childless, she would soon need to make a decision regarding her biological clock, a situation that Bobby knew would clearly necessitate a further commitment by him if the relationship were to continue.

Bobby was at something of an impasse. He was aware that all three of these women, each desirable in their ways, were waiting for him to make a decision regarding them so that they could get on with their lives. Not that he had been holding out promises to any of them; but he knew, nevertheless, the choice was, for the moment, his.

Bobby decided that what he needed to do was take a holiday. He had some good friends in the South who had been inviting him to visit for years to go fishing, and he called them, asking if now was a good time for them to have him. They told Bobby to come ahead. "I want to get away from everything," he told his friend Ned. Ned laughed and replied, "All any of us can do is go from something to something else. But come on down, anyway."

Once he was with Ned and Larry at Larry's house on the river, Bobby Newby felt more alone than ever. Despite his old pals' conviviality and genuine enthusiasm at seeing him, Bobby began to think that Kafka had been correct in his assessment of the human condition. There were no more satisfactory answers in life than there would be in death. Regarding his—and, perhaps, Kafka's dilemma with women, Bobby understood that he would never be able to satisfy what they perceived as their needs, that nobody could. Suddenly, Bobby felt better, and he started to relax. Even Kafka, he thought, must have now and again taken a moment of comfort in the realization that one was at both the beginning and the end of consciousness responsible only for one's own life. At least there could be a painless interlude or two before the horror, as Conrad identified it, returned to spoil things for everybody.

The fishing was good. Each day aboard Larry's boat in the Gulf of Mexico Bobby caught several redfish, many in the thirty-pound range. At night he went to bed tired and happy and slept well.

The evening of the day before he was scheduled to leave, Bobby accompanied Ned and Larry to a bar downriver. It was a large, lively place named Billy's Bad Boy. Larry introduced Ned and Bobby to several patrons, all locals, one of whom was an attractive woman who looked to be about thirty-five. She had white-blonde hair cut short and perfect teeth. Her name was Verna Lee. Bobby found Verna Lee very easy to talk to; she seemed intelligent, was not too obviously flirtatious and had a ready sense of humor.

As the evening wore on, Verna Lee and Bobby found themselves deep in conversation, seated at a table apart from the others. "So what's your story, Bobby?" Verna Lee asked him. "This being our third drink together," she said, "I figure the timing's about right for you to tell it and me to hear it."

Bobby laughed, gave her a short version of his predicament and told her how the fishing was proving salutary.

"You come to a decision?" she asked.

"Only that I won't be making any sudden moves," Bobby answered. "I think it's best for me right now to take it easy on myself, let people be responsible for themselves. The situation will sort itself out even if I do nothing."

"Doing nothing is doing something," said Verna Lee. "Don't fret, Bobby, some woman's gonna come along who'll take precedence over the others. Have patience."

Verna Lee reached over and squeezed Bobby's free hand, the one that was not holding a glass, then let go.

"My turn," she said.

"Shoot."

"My marriage ended after seven years. I got hitched at eighteen, Art was twenty. I started working as a flight attendant right after the divorce. That was eleven years ago."

"You haven't remarried."

"No. I like flying and I like my independence."

"No children?"

"Not yet. It's looking doubtful."

"You're still young."

Verna Lee smiled and gave a little laugh. "Thanks, but I don't really know if I want any. My boyfriend has two daughters. They live with him and when I stay there we spend time together. Their mother's dead."

"How old are they?"

"Ten and twelve. Frank, my boyfriend, was piloting a small plane with his wife and daughters aboard. The plane crash-landed in bad weather and his wife was killed. Both girls had injuries: one broke both legs, the other lost an eye. Frank busted his hip, fractured his pelvis. His wife's neck snapped on impact."

Verna Lee got up and walked over to the bar. She returned five minutes later with two drinks, one of which she handed to Bobby. She sat down and they touched glasses and drank.

"Frank still pilots," said Verna Lee. "Bought a new Beechcraft two months ago."

"You didn't know his wife?"

"Shareen. No, I met Frank a couple of years after the accident."

"Where did you meet him?"

"On an airplane, where else?"

They both laughed.

"It's a strange life, huh?" asked Verna Lee. "If Frank hadn't had that wreck, I probably never would have met him."

"You could say that about everybody," said Bobby. "If so-and-so hadn't gone into that drugstore to buy toothpaste, he wouldn't have met that pretty cashier."

"Or the handsome pharmacist."

Bobby took a sip of his drink. "Where's your boyfriend tonight?"

"In Chicago, on business."

Verna Lee finished off most of her fourth rum and orange juice.

"I guess I'm spoiling your holiday," she said.

"What do you mean?"

"Your holiday from women."

Bobby smiled. "I like talking to you."

Verna Lee looked straight into Bobby's eyes. "Actually, Frank and I haven't been getting along so well lately."

Bobby nodded and said, "Holidays don't last forever, Verna Lee."

Life Is Like This Sometimes

: : :

Twenty-seven years ago I rode the train from Oakland, California, to Ogden, Utah, where I arrived at Sunday midnight. From there I had to catch a bus to Logan, to meet a friend. The next one was not scheduled to depart until six a.m., so I had several hours to kill in Ogden, a town I did not know.

It was late November, very cold, snow and ice on the ground. I walked into a bar full of Indians. The name of the place was Dot's Hot Spot. I took a stool and ordered a beer from the bartender, who resembled a retired Irish cop from Chicago I used to talk to at the racetrack named Eddie Dooley. Dooley had been forced to retire after the horse he'd been riding down State Street during a Saint Patrick's Day parade had collapsed from a heart attack, fallen on Eddie and crushed his right leg. One day at Sportsman's he told me he was now "takin' it out on the ponies." The last I heard of Eddie he was repairing refrigerators.

Dot's Hot Spot stayed open all night and was full of Indians who were either already drunk or about to be. During the course of the night several men slid off their stools and collapsed to the floor, where they remained undisturbed until they recovered or woke up and again took a place at the bar. The popular belief among white men was that Indians could not hold their liquor particularly well. From what I had observed by that time—I was twenty-six—neither could most white men.

I sipped my beer, listened to Charlie Rich and Freddie Fender on the Rock-ola, and kept an eye out for trouble that might be headed my way. I didn't want trouble, I just wanted to get to Logan. A white man with red hair cut short who looked to be about forty-five years old came in and sat down on the stool to my left. He ordered a shot of bar whiskey and a beer. He nodded at me.

"Looks like we're in the minority," he said.

"Oh, I don't know," I said. "I think most of these boys are drinking about the same as us."

"You got a point, hotshot," he said.

We talked for a while. His name was Rigney. I never asked if it was his first, last or only. He told me he had been up to Draper to visit his sister, who was doing a dime for armed robbery.

"She knocked down a couple or three laundromats," Rigney said, "along with her boyfriend, Walter Topper. He put Rita up to it. Hotshot jumped bail, but he can't stay disappeared forever. I'd hunt Walter Topper down and take him out of the count, Rita wanted me to."

We drank more. Rigney switched from whiskey to Tequila somewhere along in there while I nursed a few beers. I wasn't much of a drinker and I did not want to risk being kept from boarding the bus because I was drunk. I had promised to meet my friend in Logan by nine-thirty.

Rigney rolled up his shirtsleeves. Tattooed in large gothic letters on his left forearm was the name RUTH. A few Indians got into a tussle at the other end of the bar but it didn't travel. To my relief, it was a pretty quiet night in Dot's Hot Spot. Toward morning it occurred to me to ask Rigney who Ruth was.

"I don't know anybody named Ruth," he said.

We didn't talk after that except to say goodbye and good luck. At five-thirty I left the bar and went to catch a bus. Two of the Indians who had been in Dot's Hot Spot staggered into the Trailways station. The taller of the two wore a calico half-Stetson and a braid halfway down his back. He was one of the men that had been involved in the brief scuffle. A cop stopped them and ordered them to go outside and come back later when they were sober. The shorter Indian, who was hatless, passed out and slumped to the ground. His partner went out the door in a hurry. The cop picked up the Indian who had collapsed under his arms and dragged him outside.

From the window of the bus as it pulled out of Ogden I saw Rigney walking on the side of the road. It was snowing and he didn't have a coat.

A Day's Worth of Beauty

. . .

The most beautiful girl I ever saw was Princessa Paris, when she was seventeen and a half years old. I was almost seventeen when I met her. An older guy I knew from the neighborhood, Gus Argo, introduced me to Princessa—actually, she introduced herself, but Gus got me there—because he had a crush on her older sister, Turquoise, who was twenty-two. This was February of 1963, in Chicago. The street and sidewalks were coated with ice, a crust of hard, two-day-old snow covered the lawns. Princessa attended a different high school than I did, but I had heard of the Paris sisters; their beauty was legendary on the northwest side of the city.

Argo picked me up while I was walking home from the Red Hot Ranch, a diner I worked at four days a week, three afternoons after school and Saturdays. It was about eight o'clock when Gus spotted me hiking on Western Avenue. He was twenty-one and had worked at Allied Radio on Western for three years, ever since he'd graduated from high school. Argo had been a pretty good left-handed pitcher, I'd played ball with and against him a few times; he was a tough kid, and he had once backed me up in a fight. A gray and black Dodge Lancer pulled over to the curb and honked. I saw that the driver was Gus Argo, and I got in.

"Hey, Buddy, where you headed?"

"Thanks, Gus, it's freezing. To my house, I guess. I just got off work."

"Yeah, me, too, but I got to make a delivery first, drop off a hi-fi. Want to ride over with me? Won't take long."

"Sure."

"Your old lady got dinner waitin'?"

"No, she's out."

"Okay, maybe we'll get a burger and coffee at Buffalo's. I just got paid, so it's on me."

"Sounds good."

"Ever hear of the Paris sisters?"

"Yeah, everybody has. You know them?"

"I'm makin' the delivery to their house. I been tryin' to get up the nerve to ask Turquoise Paris to go out with me for two years."

"Are they really so good looking?"

"I'd give anything to spend one day with Turquoise, to have one day's worth of her beauty."

"What about the other one?"

"Princessa? She's almost eighteen, four years younger than Turquoise. I only saw her once, at the Granada on a Saturday. She's a knockout, too."

Gus cranked up the blower in the Dodge. The sky was clear black but the temperature was almost zero. The radiator in my room didn't work very well; I knew I would have to sleep with a couple of sweaters on to stay warm. Argo parked in front of the Paris house and got out.

"Come in with me," he said. "You can carry one of the boxes."

Princessa opened the front door. She was almost my height, slender and small-breasted. Her lustrous chestnut hair hung practically to her waist. Once I was inside, in the light, I took a good look at her face. She reminded me of Hedy Lamarr in *Algiers*, wearing an expression that warned a man: If you don't take care of me, someone else certainly will. Princessa's complexion was porcelain smooth; I'd never before seen skin that looked so clean.

"You can just leave the boxes on the floor in the living room," she told us. "My father will set it up when he gets home."

"Who's there, Cessa?"

Gus Argo and I looked up in the direction from which the voice asking this question had come. Gene Tierney stood at the top of the staircase. Or maybe it was Helen of Troy.

"The delivery boys," Princessa answered. "They brought the new hi-fi."

"Tell them to just leave the boxes in the living room. Daddy will set it up later."

"I just did."

The apparition on the staircase disappeared; she wasn't coming down.

"Thanks, guys," said Princessa. "I'd give you a tip but I don't have any money. I can ask Turquoise if she does."

"No," Gus said, "it's okay."

He glanced at the top of the stairs once more, then walked out of the house.

"My name is Buddy," I said to Princessa.

"Hi, Buddy," she said, and held her right hand out to me. "I'm Cessa."

I took her hand. It felt like a very small, freshly killed and skinned animal.

"Your hand is warm," I said, holding it.

"My body temperature is always slightly above normal. The doctor says people's temperatures vary."

"It feels good. Mine is cold. I wasn't wearing any gloves."

She withdrew her hand.

"Could I come back to see you sometime?" I asked.

Princessa smiled. Hedy Lamarr vanished. Princessa had one slightly crooked upper front tooth the sight of which made me want to kiss her. I smiled back, memorizing her face.

"It was nice to meet you," I said, and turned to go.

"Buddy?"

I turned around. Hedy was back.

"You can call me, if you like. My last name is Paris. I have my own phone, the number's in the book."

I went out with Princessa a couple of times. She talked about her boyfriend, who was already in college; and about Turquoise, who, Cessa told me, was a party girl.

"What's a party girl?" I asked.

"She gets fifty dollars when she goes to the powder room, sometimes more. My parents don't know."

I didn't ask any more questions about Turquoise, but I did repeat what Princessa told me to Gus Argo.

"Fifty bucks for the powder room? You're shittin' me," he said.

"Does that mean she's a prostitute? I asked him.

"I don't think so," said Argo. "More like she goes out with visiting firemen who want a good lookin' date."

"Visiting firemen?"

"Yeah, guys from out of town. Salesmen, conventioneers."

Many years later, I read Apuleius's version of the myth of Psyche and Amor. Venus, Amor's mother, was so jealous of her son's love for Psyche that she attempted to seduce Amor in an effort to convince him to destroy his lover, which he would not do. Venus even imprisoned Amor and ordered Psyche to go to the underworld and bring up a casket filled with a day's worth of beauty. Eventually, Jupiter, Amor's father, came to his son's rescue and persuaded Venus to lay off the poor girl.

I remembered Gus Argo telling me he would have done anything to have had one day's worth of Turquoise Paris's beauty. My guess is that he never got it, and I doubt that he knew the story of Psyche and Amor. Gus just didn't seem to me like the kind of guy who'd spring for the powder room.

The Peterson Fire

: : :

It was snowing the night the Peterson house burned down. Bud Peterson was seventeen then, two years older than me. Bud got out alive because his room was on the ground floor in the rear of the house. His two sisters and their parents slept upstairs, above the living room, which was where the fire started. An ember jumped from the fireplace and ignited the carpet. Bud's parents and his ten and twelve year old sisters could not get down the staircase. When they tried to go back up, they were trapped and burned alive. There was nothing Bud Peterson could have done to save any of them. He was lucky, a fireman said, to have survived by crawling out his bedroom window.

I didn't see the house until the next afternoon. Snow flurries mixed with the ashes. Most of the structure was gone, only part of the first floor remained, and the chimney. I was surprised to see Bud Peterson standing in the street with his pals, staring at the ruins. Bud was a tall, thin boy, with almost colorless hair. He wore a Navy pea coat but no hat. Black ash was swirling around and some of it had fallen on his head. Nobody was saying much. There were about twenty of us, kids from the neighborhood, standing on the sidewalk or in the street, looking at what was left of the Peterson house.

I had walked over by myself after school to see it. Big Frank had told me about the fire in Cap's that morning when we were buying Bismarcks. Frank's brother, Otto, was a fireman. Frank said Otto had awakened him at five-thirty and asked if Frank knew Bud Peterson. Frank told him he did and Otto said, "His house burned down last night. Everybody but him is dead."

I heard somebody laugh. A couple of Bud's friends were whispering to each other and trying not to laugh but one of them couldn't help himself. I looked at Peterson but he didn't seem to mind. I remembered that he was a little goofy, maybe not too bright, but a good guy. He always seemed like one of those kids who just went along with the gang, who never really stood out. A bigger kid I didn't know came up to Bud and patted him on the left shoulder, then said something I couldn't hear. Peterson smiled a little and nodded his head. Snow started to come down harder. I put up the hood of my coat. We all just kept looking at the burned down house.

A black and white drove up and we moved aside. It stopped and a cop got out and said a few words to Bud Peterson. Bud got into the back seat of the squad car with the cop and the car drove away. The sky was getting dark pretty fast and the crowd broke up.

One of Bud's sisters, Irma, the one who was twelve, had a dog, a brown and black mutt. I couldn't remember its name. Nobody had said anything about Irma's dog, if it got out alive or not. I used to see her walking that dog when I was coming home from baseball or football practice.

Bud Peterson went to live with a relative. Once in a while, in the first few weeks after the fire, I would see him back in the neighborhood, hanging out with the guys, then I didn't see him anymore. Somebody said he'd moved away from Chicago.

One morning, more than thirty years later, I was sitting at a bar in Paris drinking a coffee when, for no particular reason, I thought about standing in front of the Peterson house that afternoon and wondering: If it had been snowing hard enough the night before, could the snow have put out the fire? Then I remembered the name of Irma Peterson's dog.

Books by Barry Gifford

FICTION

Do the Blind Dream?
American Falls: The Collected Short Stories
Wyoming
My Last Martini
The Sinaloa Story
Baby Cat-Face
Arise and Walk
Night People
Port Tropique
Landscape with Traveler
A Boy's Novel
The Sailor & Lula Novels:
    Wild at Heart
    Perdita Durango
    Sailor's Holiday
    Sultans of Africa
    Consuelo's Kiss
    Bad Day for the Leopard Man

NONFICTION

Out of the Past: Adventures in Film Noir
Las Cuatro Reinas (with David Perry)
Bordertown (with David Perry)
The Phantom Father: A Memoir
A Day at the Races: The Education of a Racetracker
Saroyan: A Biography (with Lawrence Lee)
The Neighborhood of Baseball
Jack's Book: An Oral Biography of Jack Kerouac (with Lawrence Lee)
Brando Rides Alone

POETRY

Back in America
Replies to Wang Wei
Ghosts No Horse Can Carry
Giotto's Circle
Flaubert at Key West
Beautiful Phantoms
Horse hauling timber out of Hokkaido forest
Poems from Snail Hut
Persimmon: Poems for Paintings
Selected Poems of Francis Jammes (translations with Bettina Dickie)
The Boy You Have Always Loved
Coyote Tantras
The Blood of the Parade

PLAYS

Hotel Room Trilogy

SCREENPLAY

Lost Highway (with David Lynch)

ANTHOLOGY

The Rooster Trapped in the Reptile Room: A Barry Gifford Reader

About the Author

Barry Gifford's novels have been translated into twenty-five languages. His book *Night People* was awarded the Premio Brancati in Italy, and he has been the recipient of awards from PEN, the National Endowment for the Arts, the American Library Association, and the Writers Guild of America. David Lynch's film *Wild at Heart*, which was based on Gifford's novel, won the Palme d'Or at the Cannes Film Festival in 1990; Gifford's novel *Perdita Durango* was made into a feature film by Spanish director Alex de la Iglesia in 1997. Gifford cowrote with director David Lynch the film *Lost Highway* (1997) and cowrote with director Matt Dillon the film *City of Ghosts* (2003). Gifford's recent books include *The Phantom Father*, named a *New York Times* Notable Book of the Year; *Wyoming*, named a *Los Angeles Times* Novel of the Year; *American Falls: The Collected Short Stories*; and *The Rooster Trapped in the Reptile Room: A Barry Gifford Reader*. His writings have appeared in *Punch*, *Esquire*, *Rolling Stone*, *Sport*, the *New York Times*, *El País*, *Reforma*, *La Repubblica*, *Projections*, and many other publications. He lives in the San Francisco Bay Area. Visit www.barrygifford.com for more information.